DOVER·THRIFT·EDITIONS

Richard III

WILLIAM SHAKESPEARE

DOVER PUBLICATIONS, INC.
New York

DOVER THRIFT EDITIONS

GENERAL EDITOR: STANLEY APPELBAUM
EDITOR OF THIS VOLUME: CANDACE WARD

Published in Canada by General Publishing Company, Ltd., 30 Lesmill Road, Don Mills, Toronto, Ontario.
Published in the United Kingdom by Constable and Company, Ltd., 3 The Lanchesters, 162–164 Fulham Palace Road, London W6 9ER.

Theatrical Rights

This Dover Thrift Edition may be used in its entirety, adaptation or in any other way for theatrical productions and performances, professional and amateur, without fee, permission or acknowledgment.

Bibliographical Note

This Dover edition, first published in 1995, contains the unabridged text of *Richard III* as published in Volume X of *The Caxton Edition of the Complete Works of William Shakespeăre*, Caxton Publishing Company, London, n.d. The Note was prepared specially for this edition, and explanatory footnotes from the Caxton edition have been supplemented and revised.

Library of Congress Cataloging-in-Publication Data

Shakespeare, William, 1564–1616.
    [King Richard III]
    Richard III / William Shakespeare.
        p.   cm. — (Dover thrift editions)
    ISBN 0-486-28747-5 (pbk.)
    1. Richard III, King of England, 1452–1485—Drama.   2. Great Britain—Kings and rulers—Drama.   I. Title.   II. Series.
PR2821.A1   1995
822.3'3—dc20   95-39598
                                                                             CIP

Manufactured in the United States of America
Dover Publications, Inc., 31 East 2nd Street, Mineola, N.Y. 11501

Note

Richard III was probably written between 1592 and 1593, soon after Shakespeare completed the three Henry VI plays. Shakespeare's primary source for the play's historical events was the 1587 edition of Raphael Holinshed's *Chronicles of England, Scotland and Ireland,* and the basis of his information on Richard was Sir Thomas More's *The Life of Richard III* (1513). More's portrayal of a villainous, deformed Richard is hardly surprising. Henry VIII, whom More served, was the son of Henry Tudor, the Lancastrian claimant to the crown who defeated Richard at the Battle of Bosworth Field and assumed the throne as Henry VII. (Henry's accession effectively ended the long and bloody dynastic civil wars known as the Wars of the Roses [1455–85].)

Despite the character's basis in sixteenth-century propaganda, Shakespeare's fictional Richard is better known than the historical figure. Ruthless and ambitious, the hunchbacked king vies with Iago in his depravity. Richard's political machinations exceed even those of Machiavelli, whom, as he boasts in *3 Henry VI,* he will "set . . . to school" (III. ii. 193). Richard's deformed soul is matched by his deformed physiognomy—he is a "poisonous bunch-backed toad," an "elvish-mark'd, abortive rooting hog," "hell's black intelligencer." But Richard flaunts his physical appearance as readily as his malevolence. Since, as he says in his opening soliloquy, he is not "made to court an amorous looking-glass," he is "determined to prove a villain," a royal deceiver, a plotter extraordinaire. He becomes all this and more—one of Shakespeare's most memorable villains.

Contents

DRAMATIS PERSONÆ   v

ACT I   1

ACT II   30

ACT III   42

ACT IV   67

ACT V   92

Dramatis Personæ

KING EDWARD the Fourth.

EDWARD, Prince of Wales, afterwards King Edward V, ⎱ sons to
RICHARD, Duke of York. ⎰ the King.

GEORGE, Duke of Clarence,
RICHARD, Duke of Gloucester, afterwards ⎱ brothers to the King.
    King Richard III. ⎰

A young son of Clarence.

HENRY, Earl of Richmond, afterwards King Henry VII.

CARDINAL BOURCHIER, Archbishop of Canterbury.

THOMAS ROTHERHAM, Archbishop of York.

JOHN MORTON, Bishop of Ely.

DUKE OF BUCKINGHAM.

DUKE OF NORFOLK.

EARL OF SURREY, his son.

EARL RIVERS, brother to Elizabeth.

MARQUIS OF DORSET and LORD GREY, sons to Elizabeth.

EARL OF OXFORD.

LORD HASTINGS.

LORD STANLEY, called also EARL OF DERBY.

LORD LOVEL.

SIR THOMAS VAUGHAN.

SIR RICHARD RATCLIFF.

SIR WILLIAM CATESBY.

SIR JAMES TYRREL.

SIR JAMES BLOUNT.

SIR WALTER HERBERT.

SIR ROBERT BRAKENBURY, Lieutenant of the Tower.

SIR WILLIAM BRANDON.

CHRISTOPHER URSWICK, a priest.

Another Priest.

TRESSEL and BERKELEY, gentlemen attending on the Lady Anne.
Lord Mayor of London.
Sheriff of Wiltshire.

ELIZABETH, queen to King Edward IV.
MARGARET, widow of King Henry VI.
DUCHESS OF YORK, mother to King Edward IV.
LADY ANNE, widow of Edward Prince of Wales, son to King Henry VI;
    afterwards married to Richard.
A young daughter of Clarence (MARGARET PLANTAGENET).

Ghosts of those murdered by Richard III, Lords and other Attendants; a
    Pursuivant, Scrivener, Citizens, Murderers, Messengers, Soldiers, &c.

SCENE: *England*

ACT I.

SCENE I. *London. A Street.*

Enter RICHARD, DUKE OF GLOUCESTER, *solus*

GLOU.   Now is the winter of our discontent
    Made glorious summer by this sun of York;[1]
    And all the clouds that lour'd upon our house
    In the deep bosom of the ocean buried.
    Now are our brows bound with victorious wreaths;
    Our bruised arms hung up for monuments;
    Our stern alarums changed to merry meetings,
    Our dreadful marches to delightful measures.
    Grim-visaged war hath smooth'd his wrinkled front;
    And now, instead of mounting barbed[2] steeds
    To fright the souls of fearful adversaries,
    He capers nimbly in a lady's chamber
    To the lascivious pleasing of a lute.
    But I, that am not shaped for sportive tricks,
    Nor made to court an amorous looking-glass;
    I, that am rudely stamp'd, and want love's majesty
    To strut before a wanton ambling nymph;
    I, that am curtail'd of this fair proportion,[3]
    Cheated of feature by dissembling nature,[4]
    Deform'd, unfinish'd, sent before my time
    Into this breathing world, scarce half made up,
    And that so lamely and unfashionable
    That dogs bark at me as I halt by them;

---

1. *this sun of York*] a punning reference to the badge of the "blazing sun" adopted by Edward IV.
2. *barbed*] caparisoned with warlike trappings.
3. *this fair proportion*] the fair shape (which "serves love's majesty," two lines above).
4. *Cheated . . . nature*] robbed of attractive figure by distorting nature.

1

Why, I, in this weak piping time of peace,[5]
Have no delight to pass away the time,
Unless to spy my shadow in the sun,
And descant on mine own deformity:
And therefore, since I cannot prove a lover,
To entertain these fair well-spoken days,[6]
I am determined to prove a villain,
And hate the idle pleasures of these days.
Plots have I laid, inductions[7] dangerous,
By drunken prophecies, libels and dreams,
To set my brother Clarence and the king
In deadly hate the one against the other:
And if King Edward be as true and just
As I am subtle, false and treacherous,
This day should Clarence closely be mew'd up,[8]
About a prophecy, which says that G
Of Edward's heirs the murderer shall be.
Dive, thoughts, down to my soul: here Clarence comes.[9]

Enter CLARENCE, *guarded, and* BRAKENBURY

Brother, good day: what means this armed guard
That waits upon your grace?
CLAR.   His majesty,
Tendering[10] my person's safety, hath appointed
This conduct[11] to convey me to the Tower.
GLOU.   Upon what cause?
CLAR.   Because my name is George.
GLOU.   Alack, my lord, that fault is none of yours;
He should, for that, commit your godfathers:
O, belike his majesty hath some intent
That you shall be new-christen'd in the Tower.
But what's the matter, Clarence? may I know?
CLAR.   Yea, Richard, when I know; for I protest
As yet I do not: but, as I can learn,
He hearkens after prophecies and dreams;

---

5. *piping time of peace*] The pipe and tabor were usual emblems of peace, as the drum and fife were of war.
6. *these fair . . . days*] these happy, prosperous days.
7. *inductions*] preparatory steps, groundwork.
8. *mew'd up*] confined.
9. *a prophecy . . . comes*] G is the initial of Clarence's Christian name George (under which he is listed in the *Dramatis Personae*). King Edward purportedly was greatly disturbed by a prophecy that Edward would be succeeded by someone whose name began with "G."
10. *Tendering*] having tender regard for.
11. *conduct*] escort.

And from the cross-row[12] plucks the letter G,
And says a wizard told him that by G
His issue disinherited should be;
And, for my name of George begins with G,
It follows in his thought that I am he.
These, as I learn, and such like toys as these
Have moved his highness to commit me now.

GLOU.   Why, this it is, when men are ruled by women:
'Tis not the king that sends you to the Tower;
My Lady Grey his wife, Clarence, 'tis she
That tempers[13] him to this extremity.
Was it not she and that good man of worship,
Anthony Woodville, her brother there,
That made him send Lord Hastings to the Tower,
From whence this present day he is deliver'd?
We are not safe, Clarence; we are not safe.

CLAR.   By heaven, I think there's no man is secure,
But the queen's kindred and night-walking heralds,
That trudge betwixt the king and Mistress Shore.
Heard ye not what an humble suppliant
Lord Hastings was to her for his delivery?

GLOU.   Humbly complaining to her deity
Got my lord chamberlain his liberty.
I'll tell you what; I think it is our way,
If we will keep in favour with the king,
To be her men and wear her livery:
The jealous o'erworn widow and herself,[14]
Since that our brother dubb'd them gentlewomen,
Are mighty gossips in this monarchy.

BRAK.   I beseech your graces both to pardon me;
His majesty hath straitly given in charge
That no man shall have private conference,
Of what degree soever, with his brother.

GLOU.   Even so; an 't please your worship, Brakenbury,
You may partake of any thing we say:
We speak no treason, man: we say the king
Is wise and virtuous, and his noble queen
Well struck in years, fair, and not jealous;

---

12. *cross-row*] alphabet; more frequently called "criss-cross-row." "Criss-cross" is a corruption of "Christ's cross," the prayer "Christ's cross be my speed" commonly standing at the head of the alphabet as printed in the elementary school books of the day.
13. *tempers*] frames or disposes.
14. *o'erworn widow and herself*] Edward IV's Queen and Jane Shore, his mistress. Though the latter was influential for a time, after Edward's death she was imprisoned for witchcraft and later died in poverty.

We say that Shore's wife hath a pretty foot,
A cherry lip, a bonny eye, a passing pleasing tongue;
And that the queen's kindred are made gentle-folks:
How say you, sir? can you deny all this?

BRAK.   With this, my lord, myself have nought to do.

GLOU.   Naught to do with Mistress Shore! I tell thee, fellow,
He that doth naught[15] with her, excepting one,
Were best he do it secretly alone.

BRAK.   What one, my lord?

GLOU.   Her husband, knave: wouldst thou betray me?

BRAK.   I beseech your grace to pardon me, and withal
Forbear your conference with the noble duke.

CLAR.   We know thy charge, Brakenbury, and will obey.

GLOU.   We are the queen's abjects,[16] and must obey.
Brother, farewell: I will unto the king;
And whatsoever you will employ me in,
Were it to call King Edward's widow sister,
I will perform it to enfranchise you.
Meantime, this deep disgrace in brotherhood
Touches me deeper than you can imagine.

CLAR.   I know it pleaseth neither of us well.

GLOU.   Well, your imprisonment shall not be long;
I will deliver you, or else lie for you:[17]
Meantime, have patience.

CLAR.   I must perforce. Farewell.

[*Exeunt* CLARENCE, BRAKENBURY, *and* Guard.]

GLOU.   Go tread the path that thou shalt ne'er return,
Simple, plain Clarence! I do love thee so,
That I will shortly send thy soul to heaven,
If heaven will take the present at our hands.
But who comes here? the new-deliver'd Hastings?

Enter LORD HASTINGS

HAST.   Good time of day unto my gracious lord!

GLOU.   As much unto my good lord chamberlain!
Well are you welcome to the open air.
How hath your lordship brook'd imprisonment?

HAST.   With patience, noble lord, as prisoners must:
But I shall live, my lord, to give them thanks
That were the cause of my imprisonment.

---

15. *Naught . . . naught*] a quibble between "nought," i.e., nothing, and "naught," i.e., naughtily.
16. *abjects*] base slaves, the scum of the people.
17. *lie for you*] lie imprisoned in your stead.

GLOU.   No doubt, no doubt; and so shall Clarence too;
      For they that were your enemies are his,
      And have prevail'd as much on him[18] as you.
HAST.   More pity that the eagle should be mew'd,[19]
      While kites and buzzards prey at liberty.
GLOU.   What news abroad?
HAST.   No news so bad abroad as this at home;
      The king is sickly, weak and melancholy,
      And his physicians fear him[20] mightily.
GLOU.   Now, by Saint Paul, this news is bad indeed.
      O, he hath kept an evil diet long,
      And overmuch consumed his royal person:
      'Tis very grievous to be thought upon.
      What, is he in his bed?
HAST.   He is.
GLOU.   Go you before, and I will follow you.   [*Exit* HASTINGS.]
      He cannot live, I hope; and must not die,
      Till George be pack'd with post-horse up to heaven.
      I'll in, to urge his hatred more to Clarence,
      With lies well steel'd with weighty arguments;
      And, if I fail not in my deep intent,
      Clarence hath not another day to live:
      Which done, God take King Edward to his mercy,
      And leave the world for me to bustle in!
      For then I'll marry Warwick's youngest daughter.[21]
      What though I kill'd her husband and her father?
      The readiest way to make the wench amends
      Is to become her husband and her father:
      The which will I, not all so much for love,
      As for another secret close intent,
      By marrying her which I must reach unto.
      But yet I run before my horse to market:
      Clarence still breathes; Edward still lives and reigns:
      When they are gone, then must I count my gains.   [*Exit.*]

---

18. *on him*] against him.
19. *mew'd*] hawks were "mewed" or kept in confinement while moulting.
20. *fear him*] fear for, are anxious about, him.
21. *Warwick's youngest daughter*] Anne, younger daughter of the Earl of Warwick, had
      been affianced (rather than actually married) to Queen Margaret and Henry VI's son,
      Edward, Prince of Wales, who was slain at the battle of Tewkesbury, May 4, 1471.

SCENE II. *The Same. Another Street*

Enter the corpse of KING HENRY THE SIXTH, Gentlemen *with halberds*[1] *to guard it;* LADY ANNE *being the mourner*

ANNE.   Set down, set down your honourable load —
    If honour may be shrouded in a hearse —
    Whilst I awhile obsequiously lament
    The untimely fall of virtuous Lancaster.
    Poor key-cold[2] figure of a holy king!
    Pale ashes of the house of Lancaster!
    Thou bloodless remnant of that royal blood!
    Be it lawful that I invocate thy ghost,
    To hear the lamentations of poor Anne,
    Wife to thy Edward, to thy slaughtered son,
    Stabb'd by the selfsame hand that made these wounds!
    Lo, in these windows that let forth thy life
    I pour the helpless balm of my poor eyes.
    Cursed be the hand that made these fatal holes!
    Cursed be the heart that had the heart to do it!
    Cursed the blood that let this blood from hence!
    More direful hap[3] betide that hated wretch,
    That makes us wretched by the death of thee,
    Than I can wish to adders, spiders, toads,
    Or any creeping venom'd thing that lives!
    If ever he have child, abortive be it,
    Prodigious,[4] and untimely brought to light,
    Whose ugly and unnatural aspect
    May fright the hopeful mother at the view;
    And that be heir to his unhappiness!
    If ever he have wife, let her be made
    As miserable by the death of him,
    As I am made by my poor lord and thee!
    Come, now towards Chertsey[5] with your holy load,
    Taken from Paul's[6] to be interred there;
    And still, as you are weary of the weight,

---

1. *halberds*] battle-axes fitted to long poles.
2. *key-cold*] cold as a key; in common use as an intensitive of "cold."
3. *hap*] fortune.
4. *Prodigious*] like a prodigy or monster.
5. *Chertsey*] a monastery near London.
6. *Paul's*] St. Paul's Church, the principal cathedral in London.

Rest you, whiles I lament King Henry's corse.[7]

Enter GLOUCESTER

GLOU.   Stay, you that bear the corse, and set it down.
ANNE.   What black magician conjures up this fiend,
    To stop devoted charitable deeds?
GLOU.   Villains, set down the corse; or, by Saint Paul,
    I'll make a corse of him that disobeys.
GENT.   My lord, stand back, and let the coffin pass.
GLOU.   Unmanner'd dog! stand thou, when I command:
    Advance thy halberd higher than my breast,
    Or, by Saint Paul, I'll strike thee to my foot,
    And spurn upon thee, beggar, for thy boldness.
ANNE.   What, do you tremble? are you all afraid?
    Alas, I blame you not; for you are mortal,
    And mortal eyes cannot endure the devil.
    Avaunt, thou dreadful minister of hell!
    Thou hadst but power over his mortal body,
    His soul thou canst not have; therefore, be gone.
GLOU.   Sweet saint, for charity, be not so curst.
ANNE.   Foul devil, for God's sake, hence, and trouble us not;
    For thou hast made the happy earth thy hell,
    Fill'd it with cursing cries and deep exclaims.
    If thou delight to view thy heinous deeds,
    Behold this pattern of thy butcheries.
    O, gentlemen, see, see! dead Henry's wounds
    Open their congeal'd mouths and bleed afresh.
    Blush, blush, thou lump of foul deformity;
    For 'tis thy presence that exhales[8] this blood
    From cold and empty veins, where no blood dwells;
    Thy deed, inhuman and unnatural,
    Provokes this deluge most unnatural.
    O God, which this blood madest, revenge his death!
    O earth, which this blood drink'st, revenge his death!
    Either heaven with lightning strike the murderer dead,
    Or earth, gape open wide and eat him quick,[9]
    As thou dost swallow up this good king's blood,
    Which his hell-govern'd arm hath butchered!
GLOU.   Lady, you know no rules of charity,
    Which renders good for bad, blessings for curses.

---

7. *corse*] corpse.
8. *exhales*] draws forth. It was a popular notion that a murdered corpse bled in presence of
the murderer.
9. *quick*] alive.

ANNE.   Villain, thou know'st no law of God nor man:
   No beast so fierce but knows some touch of pity.
GLOU.   But I know none, and therefore am no beast.
ANNE.   O wonderful, when devils tell the truth!
GLOU.   More wonderful, when angels are so angry.
   Vouchsafe, divine perfection of a woman,
   Of these supposed evils, to give me leave,
   By circumstance,[10] but to acquit myself.
ANNE.   Vouchsafe, defused[11] infection of a man,
   For these known evils, but to give me leave,
   By circumstance, to curse thy cursed self.
GLOU.   Fairer than tongue can name thee, let me have
   Some patient leisure to excuse myself.
ANNE.   Fouler than heart can think thee, thou canst make
   No excuse current,[12] but to hang thyself.
GLOU.   By such despair, I should accuse myself.
ANNE.   And, by despairing, shouldst thou stand excused
   For doing worthy vengeance on thyself,
   Which didst unworthy slaughter upon others.
GLOU.   Say that I slew them not?
ANNE.   Why, then they are not dead:
   But dead they are, and, devilish slave, by thee.
GLOU.   I did not kill your husband.
ANNE.   Why, then he is alive.
GLOU.   Nay, he is dead; and slain by Edward's hand.
ANNE.   In thy foul throat thou liest: Queen Margaret saw
   Thy murderous falchion[13] smoking in his blood;
   The which thou once didst bend against her breast,
   But that thy brothers beat aside the point.
GLOU.   I was provoked by her slanderous tongue,
   Which laid their guilt upon my guiltless shoulders.
ANNE.   Thou wast provoked by thy bloody mind,
   Which never dreamt on aught but butcheries:
   Didst thou not kill this king?
GLOU.   I grant ye.
ANNE.   Dost grant me, hedgehog? then, God grant me too
   Thou mayst be damned for that wicked deed!
   O, he was gentle, mild, and virtuous!
GLOU.   The fitter for the King of heaven, that hath him.
ANNE.   He is in heaven, where thou shalt never come.

---

10. *circumstance*] circumstantial detail.
11. *defused*] uncouthly spread, shapeless.
12. *current*] having currency, worth.
13. *falchion*] scimitar.

GLOU.   Let him thank me, that holp to send him thither;
  For he was fitter for that place than earth.
ANNE.   And thou unfit for any place but hell.
GLOU.   Yes, one place else, if you will hear me name it.
ANNE.   Some dungeon.
GLOU.   Your bed-chamber.
ANNE.   Ill rest betide the chamber where thou liest!
GLOU.   So will it, madam, till I lie with you.
ANNE.   I hope so.
GLOU.   I know so. But, gentle Lady Anne,
  To leave this keen encounter of our wits,
  And fall somewhat into a slower method,
  Is not the causer of the timeless[14] deaths
  Of these Plantagenets, Henry and Edward,
  As blameful as the executioner?
ANNE.   Thou art the cause, and most accursed effect.[15]
GLOU.   Your beauty was the cause of that effect;
  Your beauty, which did haunt me in my sleep
  To undertake the death of all the world,
  So I might live one hour in your sweet bosom.
ANNE.   If I thought that, I tell thee, homicide,
  These nails should rend that beauty from my cheeks.
GLOU.   These eyes could never endure sweet beauty's wreck;
  You should not blemish it, if I stood by:
  As all the world is cheered by the sun,
  So I by that; it is my day, my life.
ANNE.   Black night o'ershade thy day, and death thy life!
GLOU.   Curse not thyself, fair creature; thou art both.
ANNE.   I would I were, to be revenged on thee.
GLOU.   It is a quarrel most unnatural,
  To be revenged on him that loveth you.
ANNE.   It is a quarrel just and reasonable,
  To be revenged on him that slew my husband.
GLOU.   He that bereft thee, lady, of thy husband,
  Did it to help thee to a better husband.
ANNE.   His better doth not breathe upon the earth.
GLOU.   He lives that loves you better than he could.
ANNE.   Name him.
GLOU.   Plantagenet.
ANNE.   Why, that was he.
GLOU.   The selfsame name, but one of better nature.

---

14. *timeless*] untimely.
15. *effect*] effecter, doer, executioner. The act is put for the agent. In the next line "effect"
  is employed in the ordinary manner, and means "the deaths of these Plantagenets."

ANNE.   Where is he?
GLOU.   Here. [*She spitteth at him.*] Why dost thou spit at me?
ANNE.   Would it were mortal poison, for thy sake!
GLOU.   Never came poison from so sweet a place.
ANNE.   Never hung poison on a fouler toad.
     Out of my sight! thou dost infect my eyes.
GLOU.   Thine eyes, sweet lady, have infected mine.
ANNE.   Would they were basilisks,[16] to strike thee dead!
GLOU.   I would they were, that I might die at once;
     For now they kill me with a living death.
     Those eyes of thine from mine have drawn salt tears,
     Shamed their aspect with store of childish drops:
     These eyes, which never shed remorseful tear,
     No, when my father York and Edward wept,
     To hear the piteous moan that Rutland made
     When black-faced Clifford shook his sword at him;
     Nor when thy warlike father, like a child,
     Told the sad story of my father's death,
     And twenty times made pause to sob and weep,
     That all the standers-by had wet their cheeks,
     Like trees bedash'd with rain: in that sad time
     My manly eyes did scorn an humble tear;
     And what these sorrows could not thence exhale,[17]
     Thy beauty hath, and made them blind with weeping.
     I never sued to friend nor enemy;
     My tongue could never learn sweet smoothing words;
     But, now thy beauty is proposed my fee,
     My proud heart sues, and prompts my tongue to speak.
                      [*She looks scornfully at him.*]
     Teach not thy lips such scorn, for they were made
     For kissing, lady, not for such contempt.
     If thy revengeful heart cannot forgive,
     Lo, here I lend thee this sharp-pointed sword;
     Which if thou please to hide in this true bosom,
     And let the soul forth that adoreth thee,
     I lay it naked to the deadly stroke,
     And humbly beg the death upon my knee.
        [*He lays his breast open: she offers at it with his sword.*]
     Nay, do not pause; for I did kill King Henry,
     But 'twas thy beauty that provoked me.
     Nay, now dispatch; 'twas I that stabb'd young Edward,
     But 'twas thy heavenly face that set me on.

---

16. *basilisks*] fabulous reptiles who could kill with a look.
17. *exhale*] draw forth.

[Here she lets fall the sword.]
    Take up the sword again, or take up me.
ANNE.   Arise, dissembler: though I wish thy death,
    I will not be the executioner.
GLOU.   Then bid me kill myself, and I will do it.
ANNE.   I have already.
GLOU.   Tush, that was in thy rage:
    Speak it again, and, even with the word,
    That hand, which, for thy love, did kill thy love,
    Shall, for thy love, kill a far truer love;
    To both their deaths shalt thou be accessary.
ANNE.   I would I knew thy heart.
GLOU.   'Tis figured in my tongue.
ANNE.   I fear me both are false.
GLOU.   Then never man was true.
ANNE.   Well, well, put up your sword.
GLOU.   Say, then, my peace is made.
ANNE.   That shall you know hereafter.
GLOU.   But shall I live in hope?
ANNE.   All men, I hope, live so.
GLOU.   Vouchsafe to wear this ring.
ANNE.   To take is not to give.
GLOU.   Look, how this ring encompasseth thy finger,
    Even so thy breast encloseth my poor heart;
    Wear both of them, for both of them are thine.
    And if thy poor devoted suppliant may
    But beg one favour at thy gracious hand,
    Thou dost confirm his happiness for ever.
ANNE.   What is it?
GLOU.   That it would please thee leave these sad designs
    To him that hath more cause to be a mourner,
    And presently repair to Crosby Place;[18]
    Where, after I have solemnly interr'd
    At Chertsey monastery this noble king,
    And wet his grave with my repentant tears,
    I will with all expedient[19] duty see you:
    For divers unknown reasons, I beseech you,
    Grant me this boon.
ANNE.   With all my heart; and much it joys me too,

---

18. *Crosby Place*] a fine house of timber and stone in Bishopsgate Street, London, built a few years before by Sir John Crosby, a prominent citizen of London. Richard occupied it while he was Protector. The building, after undergoing successive renovations, was demolished in January, 1908.
19. *expedient*] expeditious.

    To see you are become so penitent.
    Tressel and Berkeley, go along with me.
GLOU.   Bid me farewell.
ANNE.   'Tis more than you deserve;
    But since you teach me how to flatter you,
    Imagine I have said farewell already.
              [Exeunt LADY ANNE, TRESSEL, *and* BERKELEY.*]*
GLOU.   Sirs, take up the corse.
GENT.   Towards Chertsey, noble lord?
GLOU.   No, to White-Friars;[20] there attend my coming.
                     [Exeunt all but GLOUCESTER.*]*
    Was ever woman in this humour woo'd?
    Was ever woman in this humour won?
    I'll have her; but I will not keep her long.
    What! I, that kill'd her husband and his father,
    To take[21] her in her heart's extremest hate,
    With curses in her mouth, tears in her eyes,
    The bleeding witness of her hatred by;
    Having God, her conscience, and these bars against me,
    And I nothing to back my suit at all,
    But the plain devil and dissembling looks,
    And yet to win her, all the world to nothing![22]
    Ha!
    Hath she forgot already that brave prince,
    Edward, her lord, whom I, some three months since,
    Stabb'd in my angry mood at Tewksbury?
    A sweeter and a lovelier gentleman,
    Framed in the prodigality of nature,
    Young, valiant, wise, and, no doubt, right royal,
    The spacious world cannot again afford:
    And will she yet debase her eyes on me,
    That cropp'd the golden prime of this sweet prince,
    And made her widow to a woful bed?
    On me, whose all not equals Edward's moiety?[23]
    On me, that halt and am unshapen thus?
    My dukedom to a beggarly denier,[24]

---

20. *White-Friars*] According to the 1587 edition of Holinshed's *Chronicles,* one of Shakespeare's major sources for his English history plays, the corpse was taken to the religious house of the Dominicans, in the city of London, known as Blackfriars, and not to White-Friars, a neighbouring house of the Carmelites or white friars. Districts in the city of London are still familiarly known as Blackfriars and Whitefriars.
21. *take*] capture, captivate.
22. *all the world to nothing*] the odds against me being all the world to nothing.
23. *moiety*] one of two equal parts, a half.
24. *denier*] a coin of very small value; from the Latin *denarius.*

I do mistake my person all this while:
Upon my life, she finds, although I cannot,
Myself to be a marvellous proper man.
I'll be at charges[25] for a looking-glass,
And entertain[26] some score or two of tailors,
To study fashions to adorn my body:
Since I am crept in favour with myself,
I will maintain it with some little cost.
But first I'll turn yon fellow in his grave;
And then return lamenting to my love.
Shine out, fair sun, till I have bought a glass,
That I may see my shadow as I pass.   [*Exit.*]

SCENE III. *The Palace.*

Enter QUEEN ELIZABETH, LORD RIVERS, *and* LORD GREY

RIV.   Have patience, madam: there's no doubt his majesty
         Will soon recover his accustom'd health.
GREY.   In that you brook[1] it ill, it makes him worse:
         Therefore, for God's sake, entertain good comfort,
         And cheer his grace with quick and merry words.
Q. ELIZ.   If he were dead, what would betide of me?
RIV.   No other harm but loss of such a lord.
Q. ELIZ.   The loss of such a lord includes all harm.
GREY.   The heavens have bless'd you with a goodly son,
         To be your comforter when he is gone.
Q. ELIZ.   Oh, he is young, and his minority
         Is put unto the trust of Richard Gloucester,
         A man that loves not me, nor none of you.
RIV.   Is it concluded he shall be protector?
Q. ELIZ.   It is determined, not concluded[2] yet:
         But so it must be, if the king miscarry.[3]

Enter BUCKINGHAM *and* DERBY

---

  25. *at charges*] incur costs for (a looking-glass).
  26. *entertain*] take into service.

---

  1. *brook*] bear, endure. (Here, the sense is, "If you cannot endure the King's illness, it will
     make him worse.")
  2. *determined, not concluded*] settled, but not formally recorded.
  3. *miscarry*] perish, die.

GREY.   Here come the lords of Buckingham and Derby.[4]
BUCK.   Good time of day unto your royal grace!
DER.   God make your majesty joyful as you have been!
Q. ELIZ.   The Countess Richmond,[5] good my Lord of Derby,
   To your good prayers will scarcely say amen.
   Yet, Derby, notwithstanding she's your wife,
   And loves not me, be you, good lord, assured
   I hate not you for her proud arrogance.
DER.   I do beseech you, either not believe
   The envious slanders of her false accusers;
   Or, if she be accused in true report,
   Bear with her weakness, which, I think, proceeds
   From wayward sickness, and no grounded malice.[6]
RIV.   Saw you the king to-day, my Lord of Derby?
DER.   But now the Duke of Buckingham and I
   Are come from visiting his majesty.
Q. ELIZ.   What likelihood of his amendment, lords?
BUCK.   Madam, good hope; his grace speaks cheerfully.
Q. ELIZ.   God grant him health! Did you confer with him?
BUCK.   Madam, we did: he desires to make atonement[7]
   Betwixt the Duke of Gloucester and your brothers,
   And betwixt them and my lord chamberlain;
   And sent to warn them to his royal presence.
Q. ELIZ.   Would all were well! but that will never be:
   I fear our happiness is at the highest.

Enter GLOUCESTER, HASTINGS, *and* DORSET

GLOU.   They do me wrong, and I will not endure it:
   Who are they that complain unto the king,
   That I, forsooth, am stern and love them not?
   By holy Paul, they love his grace but lightly
   That fill his ears with such dissentious rumours.
   Because I cannot flatter and speak fair,
   Smile in men's faces, smooth, deceive and cog,[8]

---

4. *Derby*] In Act III, Sc. ii, and frequently in Act IV, he is called more correctly Lord Stanley. He was Thomas, Lord Stanley, who was created first Earl of Derby by Henry VII, after Richard III's death. The premature designation of Derby is due to Shakespeare's carelessness.

5. *The Countess Richmond*] Margaret, only child of John Beaufort, first Duke of Somerset, and descendant of John of Gaunt, had married Lord Stanley as her third husband. She was mother, by her first husband, Edmund Tudor, Earl of Richmond, of King Henry VII.

6. *grounded malice*] inveterate hatred.

7. *atonement*] reconciliation.

8. *smooth . . . and cog*] cajole . . . and cheat.

Duck with French nods and apish courtesy,
I must be held a rancorous enemy.
Cannot a plain man live and think no harm,
But thus his simple truth must be abused
By silken, sly, insinuating Jacks?[9]

RIV.   To whom in all this presence speaks your grace?
GLOU.   To thee, that hast nor[10] honesty nor grace.
When have I injured thee? when done thee wrong?
Or thee? or thee? or any of your faction?
A plague upon you all! His royal person —
Whom God preserve better than you would wish! —
Cannot be quiet scarce a breathing-while,
But you must trouble him with lewd[11] complaints.

Q. ELIZ.   Brother of Gloucester, you mistake the matter.
The king, of his own royal disposition,
And not provoked by any suitor else;
Aiming, belike, at your interior[12] hatred,
Which in your outward actions shows itself
Against my kindred, brothers, and myself,
Makes him to send; that thereby he may gather
The ground of your ill-will, and to remove it.

GLOU.   I cannot tell: the world is grown so bad,
That wrens make prey where eagles dare not perch:
Since every Jack became a gentleman,
There's many a gentle person made a Jack.

Q. ELIZ.   Come, come, we know your meaning, brother Gloucester;
You envy my advancement and my friends':
God grant we never may have need of you!

GLOU.   Meantime, God grants that we have need of you:
Our brother is imprison'd by your means,
Myself disgraced, and the nobility
Held in contempt; whilst many fair promotions
Are daily given to ennoble those
That scarce, some two days since, were worth a noble.[13]

Q. ELIZ.   By Him that raised me to this careful[14] height
From that contented hap which I enjoy'd,
I never did incense his majesty
Against the Duke of Clarence, but have been

---

9. *Jacks*] contemptuous term for saucy, paltry or silly men.
10. *nor*] neither.
11. *lewd*] vulgar, ignorant.
12. *interior*] inwardly cherished.
13. *a noble*] a pun on the word in the sense of a gold coin, worth about six shillings, eight
    pence.
14. *careful*] full of care, anxiety.

An earnest advocate to plead for him.
My lord, you do me shameful injury,
Falsely to draw me in these vile suspects.[15]

GLOU.   You may deny that you were not the cause
Of my Lord Hastings' late imprisonment.

RIV.   She may, my lord, for —

GLOU.   She may, Lord Rivers! why, who knows not so?
She may do more, sir, than denying that:
She may help you to many fair preferments;
And then deny her aiding hand therein,
And lay those honours on your high deserts.
What may she not? She may, yea, marry, may she, —

RIV.   What, marry, may she?

GLOU.   What, marry, may she! marry with a king,
A bachelor, a handsome stripling too:
I wis[16] your grandam had a worser match.

Q. ELIZ.   My Lord of Gloucester, I have too long borne
Your blunt upbraidings and your bitter scoffs:
By heaven, I will acquaint his majesty
With those gross taunts I often have endured.
I had rather be a country servant-maid
Than a great queen, with this condition,
To be thus taunted, scorn'd, and baited at:

Enter QUEEN MARGARET,[17] *behind*

Small joy have I in being England's queen.

Q. MAR.   And lessen'd be that small, God, I beseech thee!
Thy honour, state and seat is due to me.

GLOU.   What! threat you me with telling of the king?
Tell him, and spare not: look, what I have said
I will avouch in presence of the king:
I dare adventure to be sent to the Tower.
'Tis time to speak; my pains[18] are quite forgot.

Q. MAR.   Out, devil! I remember them too well:
Thou slewest my husband Henry in the Tower,
And Edward, my poor son, at Tewksbury.

GLOU.   Ere you were queen, yea, or your husband king,
I was a pack-horse in his great affairs;

---

15. *suspects*] suspicions.
16. *I wis*] usually spelled I-wis, meaning surely, certainly.
17. *Queen Margaret*] Margaret of Anjou, widow of Henry VI and mother of Edward Plantagenet (1453–1471), who was killed at the Battle of Tewkesbury by Gloucester and his
brothers. She was banished in 1475 and died in France without ever returning to England. Her presence in the play is for dramatic effect and is historically inaccurate.
18. *pains*] labors.

     A weeder out of his proud adversaries,
     A liberal rewarder of his friends:
     To royalise[19] his blood I spilt mine own.
Q. MAR.   Yea, and much better blood than his or thine.
GLOU.   In all which time you and your husband Grey
     Were factious for the house of Lancaster;
     And, Rivers, so were you. Was not your husband
     In Margaret's battle at Saint Alban's slain?
     Let me put in your minds, if you forget,
     What you have been ere now, and what you are;
     Withal, what I have been, and what I am.
Q. MAR.   A murderous villain, and so still thou art.
GLOU.   Poor Clarence did forsake his father, Warwick;
     Yea, and forswore himself, — which Jesu pardon! —
Q. MAR.   Which God revenge!
GLOU.   To fight on Edward's party for the crown;
     And for his meed,[20] poor lord, he is mew'd up.
     I would to God my heart were flint, like Edward's;
     Or Edward's soft and pitiful, like mine:
     I am too childish-foolish for this world.
Q. MAR.   Hie thee to hell for shame, and leave the world,
     Thou cacodemon![21] there thy kingdom is.
RIV.   My Lord of Gloucester, in those busy days
     Which here you urge to prove us enemies,
     We follow'd then our lord, our lawful king:
     So should we you, if you should be our king.
GLOU.   If I should be! I had rather be a pedlar:
     Far be it from my heart, the thought of it!
Q. ELIZ.   As little joy, my lord, as you suppose
     You should enjoy, were you this country's king,
     As little joy may you suppose in me,
     That I enjoy, being the queen thereof.
Q. MAR.   A little joy enjoys the queen thereof;
     For I am she, and altogether joyless.
     I can no longer hold me patient.   [*Advancing.*]
     Hear me, you wrangling pirates, that fall out
     In sharing that which you have pill'd[22] from me!
     Which of you trembles not that looks on me?
     If not, that, I being queen, you bow like subjects,
     Yet that, by you deposed, you quake like rebels?
     O gentle villain, do not turn away!

---

19. *royalise*] make royal.
20. *meed*] reward.
21. *cacodemon*] evil spirit.
22. *pill'd*] pillaged, plundered.

GLOU.   Foul wrinkled witch, what makest[23] thou in my sight?
Q. MAR.   But repetition of what thou hast marr'd;
    That will I make before I let thee go.
GLOU.   Wert thou not banished on pain of death?
Q. MAR.   I was; but I do find more pain in banishment,
    Than death can yield me here by my abode.
    A husband and a son thou owest to me;
    And thou a kingdom; all of you allegiance:
    The sorrow that I have, by right is yours,
    And all the pleasures you usurp are mine.
GLOU.   The curse my noble father laid on thee,
    When thou didst crown his warlike brows with paper,
    And with thy scorns drew'st rivers from his eyes,
    And then, to dry them, gavest the duke a clout,[24]
    Steep'd in the faultless blood of pretty Rutland, —
    His curses, then from bitterness of soul
    Denounced against thee, are all fall'n upon thee;
    And God, not we, hath plagued[25] thy bloody deed.[26]
Q. ELIZ.   So just is God, to right the innocent.
HAST.   O, 'twas the foulest deed to slay that babe,[27]
    And the most merciless that e'er was heard of!
RIV.   Tyrants themselves wept when it was reported.
DOR.   No man but prophesied revenge for it.
BUCK.   Northumberland, then present, wept to see it.
Q. MAR.   What! were you snarling all before I came,
    Ready to catch each other by the throat,
    And turn you all your hatred now on me?
    Did York's dread curse prevail so much with heaven,
    That Henry's death, my lovely Edward's death,
    Their kingdom's loss, my woful banishment,
    Could all but answer for that peevish brat?
    Can curses pierce the clouds and enter heaven?
    Why, then, give way, dull clouds, to my quick curses!
    If not by war, by surfeit die your king,

---

23. *makest*] doest.
24. *clout*] cloth.
25. *plagued*] punished.
26. *When . . . bloody deed*] In 3 *Hen. VI*, I, iv, York had defeated Henry VI, who named York (rather than his own son Edward) successor to the throne. Queen Margaret, however, continued the fight against the Yorkists and eventually captured York. In the play, after taking him prisoner, Margaret and her followers taunt him and bid him weep, offering him a handkerchief stained with the blood of his youngest son, the Earl of Rutland, who was killed by Lord Clifford in the preceding battle. She then forces him to wear a paper crown and at the end of the scene she and Clifford stab him to death.
27. *babe*] i.e., Rutland. The term was sometimes used to refer to older children.

As ours by murder, to make him a king!
Edward thy son, which now is Prince of Wales,
For Edward my son, which was Prince of Wales,
Die in his youth by like untimely violence!
Thyself a queen, for me that was a queen,
Outlive thy glory, like my wretched self!
Long mayst thou live to wail thy children's loss;
And see another, as I see thee now,
Deck'd in thy rights, as thou art stall'd in mine!
Long die thy happy days before thy death;
And, after many lengthen'd hours of grief,
Die neither mother, wife, nor England's queen!
Rivers and Dorset, you were standers by,
And so wast thou, Lord Hastings, when my son
Was stabb'd with bloody daggers: God, I pray him,
That none of you may live your natural age,
But by some unlook'd accident cut off!

GLOU.   Have done thy charm, thou hateful withered hag!

Q. MAR.   And leave out thee? stay, dog, for thou shalt hear me.
If heaven have any grievous plague in store
Exceeding those that I can wish upon thee,
O, let them[28] keep it till thy sins be ripe,
And then hurl down their indignation
On thee, the troubler of the poor world's peace!
The worm of conscience still begnaw thy soul!
Thy friends suspect for traitors while thou livest,
And take deep traitors for thy dearest friends!
No sleep close up that deadly eye of thine,
Unless it be whilst some tormenting dream
Affrights thee with a hell of ugly devils!
Thou elvish-mark'd,[29] abortive, rooting hog![30]
Thou that wast seal'd in thy nativity
The slave of nature and the son of hell!
Thou slander of thy mother's heavy womb
Thou loathed issue of thy father's loins!
Thou rag of honour! thou detested —

GLOU.   Margaret.

Q. MAR.   Richard!

GLOU.   Ha!

Q. MAR.   I call thee not.

---

28. *them*] heaven; the word has a collective or plural significance.
29. *elvish-mark'd*] the common superstition that persons born with scars or deformities had
   been marked by wicked fairies or elves.
30. *hog*] Richard's heraldic blazon featured a boar.

GLOU.   I cry thee mercy then, for I had thought
     That thou hadst call'd me all these bitter names.
Q. MAR.   Why, so I did; but look'd for no reply.
     O, let me make the period to my curse!
GLOU.   'Tis done by me, and ends in "Margaret."
Q. ELIZ.   Thus have you breathed your curse against yourself.
Q. MAR.   Poor painted queen, vain flourish of my fortune!
     Why strew'st thou sugar on that bottled spider,[31]
     Whose deadly web ensnareth thee about?
     Fool, fool! thou whet'st a knife to kill thyself.
     The time will come that thou shalt wish for me
     To help thee curse that poisonous bunch-back'd toad.
HAST.   False-boding woman, end thy frantic curse,
     Lest to thy harm thou move our patience.
Q. MAR.   Foul shame upon you! you have all moved mine.
RIV.   Were you well served, you would be taught your duty.
Q. MAR.   To serve me well, you all should do me duty,
     Teach me to be your queen, and you my subjects:
     O, serve me well, and teach yourselves that duty!
DOR.   Dispute not with her; she is lunatic.
Q. MAR.   Peace, master marquess, you are malapert:[32]
     Your fire-new[33] stamp of honour is scarce current.
     O, that your young nobility could judge
     What 't were to lose it, and be miserable!
     They that stand high have many blasts to shake them;
     And if they fall, they dash themselves to pieces.
GLOU.   Good counsel, marry: learn it, learn it, marquess.
DOR.   It toucheth you, my lord, as much as me.
GLOU.   Yea, and much more: but I was born so high,
     Our aery buildeth in the cedar's top,
     And dallies with the wind and scorns the sun.
Q. MAR.   And turns the sun to shade; alas! alas!
     Witness my son, now in the shade of death;
     Whose bright out-shining beams thy cloudy wrath
     Hath in eternal darkness folded up.
     Your aery buildeth in our aery's nest.
     O God, that seest it, do not suffer it;
     As it was won with blood, lost be it so!
BUCK.   Have done! for shame, if not for charity.
Q. MAR.   Urge neither charity nor shame to me:
     Uncharitably with me have you dealt,

---

31. *bottled spider*] an exceptionally large or bottle-shaped spider.
32. *malapert*] pert, forward, saucy.
33. *fire-new*] brand-new.

And shamefully by you my hopes are butcher'd.
My charity is outrage, life my shame;
And in that shame still live my sorrow's rage!
BUCK.   Have done, have done.
Q. MAR.   O princely Buckingham, I'll kiss thy hand,
In sign of league and amity with thee:
Now fair befall thee[34] and thy noble house!
Thy garments are not spotted with our blood,
Nor thou within the compass of my curse.
BUCK.   Nor no one here; for curses never pass
The lips of those that breathe them in the air.
Q. MAR.   I'll not believe but they ascend the sky,
And there awake God's gentle-sleeping peace.
O Buckingham, take heed of yonder dog!
Look, when he fawns, he bites; and when he bites,
His venom tooth will rankle to the death:
Have not to do with him, beware of him;
Sin, death, and hell have set their marks on him,
And all their ministers attend on him.
GLOU.   What doth she say, my Lord of Buckingham?
BUCK.   Nothing that I respect, my gracious lord.
Q. MAR.   What, dost thou scorn me for my gentle counsel?
And soothe the devil that I warn thee from?
O, but remember this another day,
When he shall split thy very heart with sorrow,
And say poor Margaret was a prophetess.
Live each of you the subjects to his hate,
And he to yours, and all of you to God's!   [Exit.]
HAST.   My hair doth stand on end to hear her curses.
RIV.   And so doth mine: I muse why she's at liberty.
GLOU.   I cannot blame her: by God's holy mother,
She hath had too much wrong; and I repent
My part thereof that I have done to her.
Q. ELIZ.   I never did her any, to my knowledge.
GLOU.   But you have all the vantage of her wrong.
I was too hot to do somebody good,
That is too cold in thinking of it now.
Marry, as for Clarence, he is well repaid;
He is frank'd up[35] to fatting for his pains:
God pardon them that are the cause of it!

---

34. *fair befall thee*] good fortune attend you!
35. *frank'd up*] cooped up as in a pen or sty, which was commonly called a "frank." The
    verb is used of animals, especially hogs, being fattened for the butcher.

RIV. A virtuous and a Christian-like conclusion,
    To pray for them that have done scathe[36] to us.
GLOU. So do I ever: [*Aside*] being well advised:
    For had I cursed now, I had cursed myself.

Enter CATESBY

CATES. Madam, his majesty doth call for you;
    And for your grace; and you, my noble lords.
Q. ELIZ. Catesby, we come. Lords, will you go with us?
RIV. Madam, we will attend your grace.
                        [*Exeunt all but* GLOUCESTER.]
GLOU. I do the wrong, and first begin to brawl.
    The secret mischiefs that I set abroach[37]
    I lay unto the grievous charge of others.
    Clarence, whom I, indeed, have laid in darkness,
    I do beweep to many simple gulls;[38]
    Namely, to Hastings, Derby, Buckingham;
    And say it is the queen and her allies
    That stir the king against the duke my brother.
    Now, they believe it; and withal whet me
    To be revenged on Rivers, Vaughan, Grey:
    But then I sigh; and, with a piece of Scripture,
    Tell them that God bids us do good for evil:
    And thus I clothe my naked villany
    With old odd ends[39] stolen out of holy writ;
    And seem a saint, when most I play the devil.

Enter two Murderers

    But, soft! here come my executioners.
    How now, my hardy stout resolved mates!
    Are you now going to dispatch this deed?
FIRST MURD. We are, my lord; and come to have the warrant,
    That we may be admitted where he is.
GLOU. Well thought upon; I have it here about me.
                        [*Gives the warrant.*]
    When you have done, repair to Crosby Place.
    But, sirs, be sudden in the execution,
    Withal obdurate, do not hear him plead;
    For Clarence is well-spoken, and perhaps
    May move your hearts to pity, if you mark him.

---

36. *scathe*] injury, hurt.
37. *set abroach*] to cause, set into action, agitate.
38. *gulls*] tricks, impositions.
39. *old odd ends*] quoted tags, odds and ends.

FIRST MURD.   Tush!
    Fear not, my lord, we will not stand to prate;
    Talkers are no good doers: be assured
    We come to use our hands and not our tongues.
GLOU.   Your eyes drop millstones,[40] when fools' eyes drop tears.
    I like you, lads: about your business straight.
    Go, go, dispatch.
FIRST MURD.   We will, my noble lord.   [*Exeunt.*]

SCENE IV. *London. The Tower.*

Enter CLARENCE *and* BRAKENBURY

BRAK.   Why looks your grace so heavily to-day?
CLAR.   O, I have pass'd a miserable night,
    So full of ugly sights, of ghastly dreams,
    That, as I am a Christian faithful[1] man,
    I would not spend another such a night,
    Though 't were to buy a world of happy days,
    So full of dismal terror was the time!
BRAK.   What was your dream? I long to hear you tell it.
CLAR.   Methoughts that I had broken from the Tower,
    And was embark'd to cross to Burgundy;
    And, in my company, my brother Gloucester;
    Who from my cabin tempted me to walk
    Upon the hatches: thence we look'd toward England,
    And cited up a thousand fearful times,
    During the wars of York and Lancaster,
    That had befall'n us. As we paced along
    Upon the giddy footing of the hatches,
    Methought that Gloucester stumbled; and, in falling,
    Struck me, that thought to stay him, overboard,
    Into the tumbling billows of the main.
    Lord, Lord! methought, what pain it was to drown!
    What dreadful noise of waters in mine ears!
    What ugly sights of death within mine eyes!
    Methought I saw a thousand fearful wrecks;

---

40. *Your eyes drop millstones*] an expression very commonly applied to hard-natured persons who were not in the habit of weeping at all.

---

1. *faithful*] as opposed to "infidel."

Ten thousand men that fishes gnaw'd upon;
Wedges of gold, great anchors, heaps of pearl,
Inestimable stones, unvalued² jewels,
All scattered in the bottom of the sea:
Some lay in dead men's skulls; and in those holes
Where eyes did once inhabit, there were crept,
As 't were in scorn of eyes, reflecting gems,
Which woo'd³ the slimy bottom of the deep,
And mock'd the dead bones that lay scattered by.

BRAK. Had you such leisure in the time of death
To gaze upon the secrets of the deep?

CLAR. Methought I had; and often did I strive
To yield the ghost: but still the envious⁴ flood
Kept in my soul, and would not let it forth
To seek the empty, vast and wandering air;
But smothered it within my panting bulk,⁵
Which almost burst to belch it in the sea.

BRAK. Awaked you not with this sore agony?

CLAR. O no, my dream was lengthened after life;
O, then began the tempest to my soul,
Who pass'd, methought, the melancholy flood,
With that grim ferryman which poets write of,⁶
Unto the kingdom of perpetual night.
The first that there did greet my stranger soul,
Was my great father-in-law, renowned Warwick;
Who cried aloud, "What scourge for perjury
Can this dark monarchy afford false Clarence?"
And so he vanish'd: then came wandering by
A shadow like an angel, with bright hair
Dabbled in blood; and he squeak'd out aloud,
"Clarence is come; false, fleeting,⁷ perjured Clarence,
That stabb'd me in the field by Tewksbury:⁸
Seize on him, Furies, take him to your torments!"
With that, methoughts, a legion of foul fiends
Environ'd me about, and howled in mine ears
Such hideous cries, that with the very noise
I trembling waked, and for a season after
Could not believe but that I was in hell,

---

2. *unvalued*] invaluable.
3. *woo'd*] ogled.
4. *envious*] cruel, malicious.
5. *bulk*] body, frame, trunk.
6. *Who pass'd . . . poets write of*] a reference to the myth of Charon, the Stygian ferryman.
7. *fleeting*] wavering, inconstant.
8. *A shadow . . . Tewksbury*] the ghost of Edward Plantagenet, Prince of Wales.

Such terrible impression made the dream.
BRAK.   No marvel, my lord, though it affrighted you;
    I promise you, I am afraid to hear you tell it.
CLAR.   O Brakenbury, I have done those things,
    Which now bear evidence against my soul,
    For Edward's sake; and see how he requites me!
    O God! if my deep prayers cannot appease thee,
    But thou wilt be avenged on my misdeeds,
    Yet execute thy wrath in me alone;
    O, spare my guiltless wife[9] and my poor children!
    I pray thee, gentle keeper, stay by me;
    My soul is heavy, and I fain would sleep.
BRAK.   I will, my lord: God give your grace good rest!
                                     [CLARENCE *sleeps.*]
    Sorrow breaks seasons and reposing hours,
    Makes the night morning and the noon-tide night.
    Princes have but their titles for their glories,
    An outward honour for an inward toil;
    And, for unfelt imagination,
    They often feel a world of restless cares:[10]
    So that, betwixt their titles and low names,
    There's nothing differs but the outward fame.

Enter the two Murderers

FIRST MURD.   Ho! who's here?
BRAK.   In God's name what are you, and how came you hither?
FIRST MURD.   I would speak with Clarence, and I came hither on my
    legs.
BRAK.   Yea, are you so brief?
SEC. MURD.   O sir, it is better to be brief than tedious.
    Show him our commission; talk no more.
                                      [BRAKENBURY *reads it.*]
BRAK.   I am in this commanded to deliver
    The noble Duke of Clarence to your hands:
    I will not reason what is meant hereby,
    Because I will be guiltless of the meaning.
    Here are the keys, there sits the duke asleep:
    I'll to the king; and signify to him
    That thus I have resign'd my charge to you.

---

    9. *guiltless wife*] an historical error. Clarence's wife, Isabella Neville, the elder daughter
       of the Earl of Warwick, died December 21, 1476, long before Clarence's imprison-
       ment.
   10. *for unfelt imagination . . . cares*] In return for imaginary gratification, which does not
       touch their feeling, they often feel any amount of disturbing cares.

FIRST MURD.   Do so, it is a point of wisdom: fare you well.

[*Exit* BRAKENBURY.]

SEC. MURD.   What, shall we stab him as he sleeps?

FIRST MURD.   No; then he will say 't was done cowardly, when he wakes.

SEC. MURD.   When he wakes! why, fool, he shall never wake till the judgement-day.

FIRST MURD.   Why, then he will say we stabbed him sleeping.

SEC. MURD.   The urging of that word "judgement" hath bred a kind of remorse in me.

FIRST MURD.   What, art thou afraid?

SEC. MURD.   Not to kill him, having a warrant for it; but to be damned for killing him, from which no warrant can defend us.

FIRST MURD.   I thought thou hadst been resolute.

SEC. MURD.   So I am, to let him live.

FIRST MURD.   Back to the Duke of Gloucester, tell him so.

SEC. MURD.   I pray thee, stay a while: I hope my holy humour will change; 't was wont to hold me but while one would tell[11] twenty.

FIRST MURD.   How dost thou feel thyself now?

SEC. MURD.   Faith, some certain dregs of conscience are yet within me.

FIRST MURD.   Remember our reward, when the deed is done.

SEC. MURD.   'Zounds, he dies: I had forgot the reward.

FIRST MURD.   Where is thy conscience now?

SEC. MURD.   In the Duke of Gloucester's purse.

FIRST MURD.   So when he opens his purse to give us our reward, thy conscience flies out.

SEC. MURD.   Let it go; there's few or none will entertain it.

FIRST MURD.   How if it come to thee again?

SEC. MURD.   I'll not meddle with it: it is a dangerous thing: it makes a man a coward: a man cannot steal, but it accuseth him; he cannot swear, but it checks him; he cannot lie with his neighbour's wife, but it detects him: it is a blushing shamefast spirit that mutinies in a man's bosom; it fills one full of obstacles: it made me once restore a purse of gold, that I found; it beggars any man that keeps it: it is turned out of all towns and cities for a dangerous thing; and every man that means to live well endeavours to trust to himself and to live without it.

FIRST MURD.   'Zounds, it is even now at my elbow, persuading me not to kill the duke.

SEC. MURD.   Take the devil in thy mind, and believe him[12] not: he would insinuate with thee[13] but to make thee sigh.

---

11. *tell*] count to.
12. *him*] i.e., thy conscience.
13. *insinuate with thee*] beguile thee.

FIRST MURD.   Tut, I am strong-framed, he cannot prevail with me, I
    warrant thee.
SEC. MURD.   Spoke like a tall[14] fellow that respects his reputation.
    Come, shall we to this gear?[15]
FIRST MURD.   Take him over the costard[16] with the hilts of thy sword,
    and then we will chop[17] him in the malmsey-butt[18] in the next
    room.
SEC. MURD.   O excellent device! make a sop of him.
FIRST MURD.   Hark! he stirs: shall I strike?
SEC. MURD.   No, first let's reason with him.
CLAR.   Where art thou, keeper? give me a cup of wine.
SEC. MURD.   You shall have wine enough, my lord, anon.
CLAR.   In God's name, what art thou?
SEC. MURD.   A man, as you are.
CLAR.   But not, as I am, royal.
SEC. MURD.   Nor you, as we are, loyal.
CLAR.   Thy voice is thunder, but thy looks are humble.
SEC. MURD.   My voice is now the king's, my looks mine own.
CLAR.   How darkly and how deadly dost thou speak!
    Your eyes do menace me: why look you pale?
    Who sent you hither? Wherefore do you come?
BOTH.   To, to, to —
CLAR.   To murder me?
BOTH.   Ay, ay.
CLAR.   You scarcely have the hearts to tell me so,
    And therefore cannot have the hearts to do it.
    Wherein, my friends, have I offended you?
FIRST MURD.   Offended us you have not, but the king.
CLAR.   I shall be reconciled to him again.
SEC. MURD.   Never, my lord; therefore prepare to die.
CLAR.   Are you call'd forth from out a world of men
    To slay the innocent? What is my offence?
    Where are the evidence that do accuse me?
    What lawful quest[19] have given their verdict up
    Unto the frowning judge? or who pronounced
    The bitter sentence of poor Clarence' death?
    Before I be convict by course of law,
    To threaten me with death is most unlawful.
    I charge you, as you hope to have redemption

---

14. *tall*] bold, daring; a common usage.
15. *to this gear*] to this business.
16. *Take him over the costard*] hit him over the head.
17. *chop*] to do something with a quick motion.
18. *malmsey-butt*] a large cask of malmsey (a kind of sweet wine).
19. *quest*] inquest or trial by jury; an empanelled jury.

By Christ's dear blood shed for our grievous sins,
That you depart and lay no hands on me:
The deed you undertake is damnable.

FIRST MURD. What we will do, we do upon command.

SEC. MURD. And he that hath commanded is the king.

CLAR. Erroneous vassal! the great King of kings
Hath in the tables of his law commanded
That thou shalt do no murder: and wilt thou then
Spurn at his edict, and fulfil a man's?
Take heed; for he holds vengeance in his hands,
To hurl upon their heads that break his law.

SEC. MURD. And that same vengeance doth he hurl on thee,
For false forswearing, and for murder too:
Thou didst receive the holy sacrament,
To fight in quarrel of the house of Lancaster.

FIRST MURD. And, like a traitor to the name of God,
Didst break that vow; and with thy treacherous blade
Unrip'dst the bowels of thy sovereign's son.

SEC. MURD. Whom thou wert sworn to cherish and defend.

FIRST MURD. How canst thou urge God's dreadful law to us,
When thou hast broke it in so dear degree?

CLAR. Alas! for whose sake did I that ill deed?
For Edward, for my brother, for his sake:
Why, sirs,
He sends ye not to murder me for this;
For in this sin he is as deep as I.
If God will be revenged for this deed,
O, know you yet, he doth it publicly:
Take not the quarrel from his powerful arm;
He needs no indirect nor lawless course
To cut off those that have offended him.

FIRST MURD. Who made thee then a bloody minister,
When gallant-springing[20] brave Plantagenet,
That princely novice, was struck dead by thee?

CLAR. My brother's love, the devil, and my rage.

FIRST MURD. Thy brother's love, our duty, and thy fault,
Provoke us hither now to slaughter thee.

CLAR. Oh, if you love my brother, hate not me;
I am his brother, and I love him well.
If you be hired for meed, go back again,
And I will send you to my brother Gloucester,
Who shall reward you better for my life,
Than Edward will for tidings of my death.

---

20. *gallant-springing*] like a gallant in the spring of life.

SEC. MURD.   You are deceived, your brother Gloucester hates you.
CLAR.   O, no, he loves me, and he holds me dear:
 Go you to him from me.
BOTH.   Ay, so we will.
CLAR.   Tell him, when that our princely father York
 Bless'd his three sons with his victorious arm,
 And charged us from his soul to love each other,
 He little thought of this divided friendship:
 Bid Gloucester think of this, and he will weep.
FIRST MURD.   Ay, millstones;[21] as he lesson'd us to weep.
CLAR.   O, do not slander him, for he is kind.
FIRST MURD.   Right,
 As snow in harvest. Thou deceivest thyself:
 'Tis he that sent us hither now to slaughter thee.[22]
CLAR.   It cannot be; for when I parted with him,
 He hugg'd me in his arms, and swore, with sobs,
 That he would labour my delivery.
SEC. MURD.   Why, so he doth, now he delivers thee
 From this world's thraldom to the joys of heaven.
FIRST MURD.   Make peace with God, for you must die, my lord.
CLAR.   Hast thou that holy feeling in thy soul,
 To counsel me to make my peace with God,
 And art thou yet to thy own soul so blind,
 That thou wilt war with God by murdering me?
 Ah, sirs, consider, he that set you on
 To do this deed will hate you for the deed.
SEC. MURD.   What shall we do?
CLAR.   Relent, and save your souls.
FIRST MURD.   Relent! 'tis cowardly and womanish.
CLAR.   Not to relent is beastly, savage, devilish.
 Which of you, if you were a prince's son,
 Being pent from liberty, as I am now,
 If two such murderers as yourselves came to you,
 Would not entreat for life?
 My friend, I spy some pity in thy looks;
 O, if thine eye be not a flatterer,
 Come thou on my side, and entreat for me,
 As you would beg, were you in my distress:
 A begging prince what beggar pities not?
SEC. MURD.   Look behind you, my lord.

---

21. *Ay, millstones*] see note 40, Act I, Sc. iii.
22. *'Tis ... thee*] There is no historical evidence linking Gloucester with the death of Clarence. Sixteenth-century chroniclers do report the rumour that he was drowned in a butt of malmsey.

FIRST MURD.   Take that, and that: if all this will not do,
                                                  [*Stabs him.*]
         I'll drown you in the malmsey-butt within.
                                             [*Exit, with the body.*]
SEC. MURD.   A bloody deed, and desperately dispatch'd!
         How fain, like Pilate, would I wash my hands
         Of this most grievous guilty murder done!

Re-enter First Murderer

FIRST MURD.   How now! what mean'st thou, that thou help'st me not?
         By heavens, the duke shall know how slack thou art!
SEC. MURD.   I would he knew that I had saved his brother!
         Take thou the fee, and tell him what I say;
         For I repent me that the duke is slain.   [*Exit.*]
FIRST MURD.   So do not I: go, coward as thou art.
         Now must I hide his body in some hole,
         Until the duke take order for his burial:
         And when I have my meed, I must away;
         For this will out, and here I must not stay.   [*Exit.*]

ACT II.

SCENE I. *London. The Palace.*

Flourish. Enter KING EDWARD *sick,* QUEEN ELIZABETH, DORSET, RIVERS, HASTINGS, BUCKINGHAM, GREY, *and others*

K. EDW.   Why, so: now have I done a good day's work:
         You peers, continue this united league:
         I every day expect an embassage
         From my Redeemer to redeem me hence;
         And now in peace my soul shall part[1] to heaven,
         Since I have set my friends at peace on earth.
         Rivers and Hastings, take each other's hand;
         Dissemble not your hatred, swear your love.
RIV.   By heaven, my soul is purged from grudging hate;
         And with my hand I seal my true heart's love.
HAST.   So thrive I, as I truly swear the like!
K. EDW.   Take heed you dally not before your king;

---

1. *part*] depart.

      Lest he that is the supreme King of kings
      Confound² your hidden falsehood, and award
      Either of you to be the other's end.
HAST.   So prosper I, as I swear perfect love!
RIV.   And I, as I love Hastings with my heart!
K. EDW.   Madam, yourself are not exempt in this,
      Nor your son Dorset; Buckingham, nor you;
      You have been factious one against the other.
      Wife, love Lord Hastings, let him kiss your hand;
      And what you do, do it unfeignedly.
Q. ELIZ.   Here, Hastings; I will never more remember
      Our former hatred, so thrive I and mine!
K. EDW.   Dorset, embrace him; Hastings, love lord marquess.
DOR.   This interchange of love, I here protest,
      Upon my part shall be unviolable.
HAST.   And so swear I, my lord.   [*They embrace.*]
K. EDW.   Now, princely Buckingham, seal thou this league
      With thy embracements to my wife's allies,
      And make me happy in your unity.
BUCK.   [*To the* QUEEN] Whenever Buckingham doth turn his hate
      On you or yours, but with all duteous love
      Doth³ cherish you and yours, God punish me
      With hate in those where I expect most love!
      When I have most need to employ a friend,
      And most assured that he is a friend,
      Deep, hollow, treacherous and full of guile,
      Be he unto me! this do I beg of God,
      When I am cold in zeal to you or yours.   [*They embrace.*]
K. EDW.   A pleasing cordial, princely Buckingham,
      Is this thy vow unto my sickly heart.
      There wanteth now our brother Gloucester here,
      To make the perfect period of this peace.
BUCK.   And, in good time, here comes the noble duke.

Enter GLOUCESTER

GLOU.   Good morrow to my sovereign king and queen;
      And, princely peers, a happy time of day!
K. EDW.   Happy indeed, as we have spent the day.
      Brother, we have done deeds of charity;
      Made peace of enmity, fair love of hate,
      Between these swelling wrong-incensed peers.

---

2. *Confound*] ruin, destroy.
3. *but . . . Doth*] and doth not.

GLOU. A blessed labour, my most sovereign liege:
  Amongst this princely heap,[4] if any here,
  By false intelligence, or wrong surmise,
  Hold me a foe;
  If I unwittingly, or in my rage,
  Have aught committed that is hardly borne
  By any in this presence, I desire
  To reconcile me to his friendly peace:
  'Tis death to me to be at enmity;
  I hate it, and desire all good men's love.
  First, madam, I entreat true peace of you,
  Which I will purchase with my duteous service;
  Of you, my noble cousin Buckingham,
  If ever any grudge were lodged between us;
  Of you, Lord Rivers, and, Lord Grey, of you,
  That all without desert have frown'd on me;
  Dukes, earls, lords, gentlemen; indeed, of all.
  I do not know that Englishman alive
  With whom my soul is any jot at odds,
  More than the infant that is born to-night:
  I thank my God for my humility.
Q. ELIZ. A holy day shall this be kept hereafter:
  I would to God all strifes were well compounded.
  My sovereign liege, I do beseech your majesty
  To take our brother Clarence to your grace.
GLOU. Why, madam, have I offer'd love for this
  To be so flouted in this royal presence?
  Who knows not that the noble duke is dead? [*They all start.*]
  You do him injury to scorn his corse.
RIV. Who knows not he is dead! who knows he is?
Q. ELIZ. All-seeing heaven, what a world is this!
BUCK. Look I so pale, Lord Dorset, as the rest?
DOR. Ay, my good lord; and no one in this presence
  But his red colour hath forsook his cheeks.
K. EDW. Is Clarence dead? the order was reversed.
GLOU. But he, poor soul, by your first order died,
  And that a winged Mercury did bear;
  Some tardy cripple bore the countermand,
  That came too lag to see him buried.
  God grant that some, less noble and less loyal,
  Nearer in bloody thoughts, but not in blood,

---

4. *heap*] throng, company.

Deserve not worse than wretched Clarence did,
And yet go current[5] from suspicion!

Enter DERBY

DER.   A boon, my sovereign, for my service done!
K. EDW.   I pray thee, peace: my soul is full of sorrow.
DER.   I will not rise, unless your highness grant.
K. EDW.   Then speak at once what is it thou demand'st.
DER.   The forfeit, sovereign, of my servant's life;
        Who slew to-day a riotous gentleman
        Lately attendant on the Duke of Norfolk.
K. EDW.   Have I a tongue to doom my brother's death,
        And shall that tongue give pardon to a slave?
        My brother slew no man; his fault was thought,
        And yet his punishment was cruel death.
        Who sued to me for him? who, in my rage,
        Kneel'd at my feet and bade me be advised?
        Who spake of brotherhood? who spake of love?
        Who told me how the poor soul did forsake
        The mighty Warwick, and did fight for me?
        Who told me, in the field by Tewksbury,
        When Oxford had me down, he rescued me,
        And said "Dear brother, live, and be a king"?
        Who told me, when we both lay in the field
        Frozen almost to death, how he did lap me
        Even in his own garments, and gave himself,
        All thin and naked, to the numb cold night?
        All this from my remembrance brutish wrath
        Sinfully pluck'd, and not a man of you
        Had so much grace to put it in my mind.
        But when your carters or your waiting-vassals
        Have done a drunken slaughter, and defaced
        The precious image of our dear Redeemer,
        You straight are on your knees for pardon, pardon;
        And I, unjustly too, must grant it you:
        But for my brother not a man would speak,
        Nor I, ungracious, speak unto myself
        For him, poor soul. The proudest of you all
        Have been beholding to him in his life;
        Yet none of you would once plead for his life.
        O God, I fear thy justice will take hold

---

5. *go current*] go as though perceived to be honest.

On me, and you, and mine, and yours for this!
Come, Hastings, help me to my closet. Oh, poor Clarence!

           [*Exeunt some with King and Queen.*]

GLOU.   This is the fruit of rashness. Mark'd you not
How that the guilty kindred of the queen
Look'd pale when they did hear of Clarence' death?
O, they did urge it still unto the king!
God will revenge it. But come, let us in,
To comfort Edward with our company.

BUCK.   We wait upon your grace.   [*Exeunt.*]

SCENE II. *The Palace.*

Enter the DUCHESS OF YORK, *with the two children of* CLARENCE

BOY.   Tell me, good grandam,[1] is our father dead?
DUCH.   No, boy.
BOY.   Why do you wring your hands, and beat your breast,
     And cry "O Clarence, my unhappy son"?
GIRL.   Why do you look on us, and shake your head,
     And call us wretches, orphans, castaways,
     If that our noble father be alive?
DUCH.   My pretty cousins,[2] you mistake me much.
     I do lament the sickness of the king,
     As loath to lose him; not your father's death;
     It were lost sorrow to wail one that's lost.
BOY.   Then, grandam, you conclude that he is dead.
     The king my uncle is to blame for this:
     God will revenge it; whom I will importune
     With daily prayers all to that effect.
GIRL.   And so will I.

---

1. *good grandam*] the widow of Richard, Duke of York, who was slain at the battle of Wakefield, 1460, and the mother of Edward IV, Richard III, and Clarence. She survived her husband thirty-five years. Her grandchildren, Clarence's son and daughter, with whom she converses in this scene, were respectively Edward Plantagenet, Earl of Warwick, who was executed by Henry VII on November 21, 1499, and the famous Margaret, Countess of Salisbury, mother of Cardinal Pole; the Countess was beheaded on Tower Hill at Henry VIII's instance on May 27, 1541.
2. *cousins*] This word was used for kinsfolk of any degree.

DUCH.   Peace, children, peace! the king doth love you well:
Incapable[3] and shallow innocents,
You cannot guess who caused your father's death.
BOY.   Grandam, we can; for my good uncle Gloucester
Told me, the king, provoked by the queen,
Devised impeachments to imprison him:
And when my uncle told me so, he wept,
And hugg'd me in his arm, and kindly kiss'd my cheek;
Bade me rely on him as on my father,
And he would love me dearly as his child.
DUCH.   Oh, that deceit should steal such gentle shapes,
And with a virtuous vizard hide foul guile!
He is my son; yea, and therein my shame;
Yet from my dugs[4] he drew not this deceit.
BOY.   Think you my uncle did dissemble, grandam?
DUCH.   Ay, boy.
BOY.   I cannot think it. Hark! what noise is this?

Enter QUEEN ELIZABETH, *with her hair about her ears;* RIVERS *and* DORSET *after her*

Q. ELIZ.   Oh, who shall hinder me to wail and weep,
To chide my fortune and torment myself?
I'll join with black despair against my soul,
And to myself become an enemy.
DUCH.   What means this scene of rude impatience?
Q. ELIZ.   To make an act[5] of tragic violence:
Edward, my lord, your son, our king, is dead.
Why grow the branches now the root is wither'd?
Why wither not the leaves the sap being gone?
If you will live, lament; if die, be brief,
That our swift-winged souls may catch the king's,
Or, like obedient subjects, follow him
To his new kingdom of perpetual rest.
DUCH.   Ah, so much interest have I in thy sorrow
As I had title in thy noble husband!
I have bewept a worthy husband's death,
And lived by looking on his images:[6]
But now two mirrors of his princely semblance
Are crack'd in pieces by malignant death,

---

3. *Incapable*] i.e., incapable of understanding.
4. *dugs*] teats.
5. *an act*] in a theatrical sense.
6. *his images*] the children who preserve his likeness.

And I for comfort have but one false glass,
Which grieves me when I see my shame in him.
Thou art a widow; yet thou art a mother,
And hast the comfort of thy children left thee:
But death hath snatch'd my husband from mine arms,
And pluck'd two crutches from my feeble limbs,
Edward and Clarence. O, what cause have I,
Thine being but a moiety of my grief,
To overgo thy plaints[7] and drown thy cries!

BOY.   Good aunt, you wept not for our father's death,
How can we aid you with our kindred tears?

GIRL.   Our fatherless distress was left unmoan'd;
Your widow-dolour likewise be unwept!

Q. ELIZ.   Give me no help in lamentation;
I am not barren to bring forth complaints:
All springs reduce[8] their currents to mine eyes,
That I, being govern'd by the watery moon,
May send forth plenteous tears to drown the world!
Oh for my husband, for my dear lord Edward!

CHIL.   Oh for our father, for our dear lord Clarence!

DUCH.   Alas for both, both mine, Edward and Clarence!

Q. ELIZ.   What stay had I but Edward? and he's gone.

CHIL.   What stay had we but Clarence? and he's gone.

DUCH.   What stays had I but they? and they are gone.

Q. ELIZ.   Was never widow had so dear a loss.

CHIL.   Were never orphans had so dear a loss.

DUCH.   Was never mother had so dear a loss.
Alas, I am the mother of these moans!
Their woes are parcell'd, mine are general.[9]
She for an Edward weeps, and so do I;
I for a Clarence weep, so doth not she:
These babes for Clarence weep, and so do I;
I for an Edward weep, so do not they:
Alas, you three, on me threefold distress'd
Pour all your tears! I am your sorrow's nurse,
And I will pamper it with lamentations.

DOR.   Comfort, dear mother: God is much displeased
That you take with unthankfulness his doing:
In common worldly things, 'tis call'd ungrateful,
With dull unwillingness to repay a debt

---

7. *overgo thy plaints*] exceed thy lamentations.
8. *reduce*] bring, lead back.
9. *Their woes . . . general*] Their woes are divided up amongst them; each has his own particular woe; my woes cover all theirs.

Which with a bounteous hand was kindly lent;
Much more to be thus opposite with heaven,
For it requires the royal debt it lent you.
RIV.   Madam, bethink you, like a careful mother,
Of the young prince your son: send straight for him;
Let him be crown'd; in him your comfort lives:
Drown desperate sorrow in dead Edward's grave,
And plant your joys in living Edward's throne.

Enter GLOUCESTER, BUCKINGHAM, DERBY, HASTINGS, *and* RATCLIFF

GLOU.   Madam, have comfort: all of us have cause
To wail the dimming of our shining star;
But none can cure their harms by wailing them.
Madam, my mother, I do cry you mercy;
I did not see your grace: humbly on my knee
I crave your blessing.
DUCH.   God bless thee, and put meekness in thy mind,
Love, charity, obedience, and true duty!
GLOU.   [*Aside*] Amen; and make me die a good old man!
That is the butt-end of a mother's blessing:
I marvel why her grace did leave it out.
BUCK.   You cloudy[10] princes and heart-sorrowing peers,
That bear this mutual heavy load of moan,
Now cheer each other in each other's love:
Though we have spent our harvest of this king,
We are to reap the harvest of his son.
The broken rancour[11] of your high-swoln hearts,
But lately splinter'd,[12] knit and join'd together,
Must gently be preserved, cherish'd, and kept:
Me seemeth good, that, with some little train,
Forthwith from Ludlow[13] the young prince[14] be fetch'd
Hither to London, to be crown'd our king.
RIV.   Why with some little train, my Lord of Buckingham?
BUCK.   Marry, my lord, lest, by a multitude,
The new-heal'd wound of malice should break out;
Which would be so much the more dangerous,

---

10. *cloudy*] sullen.
11. *broken rancour*] the rancour that has been broken and destroyed, the cessation of
rancour, the reconciliation.
12. *splinter'd*] joined together with splints.
13. *Ludlow*] As Prince of Wales, the young prince, according to established custom,
resided at Ludlow Castle on the Welsh border.
14. *the young prince*] the oldest son of Edward IV and Elizabeth Woodville, and soon to be
Edward V, king at the age of 13.

By how much the estate[15] is green and yet ungovern'd:
Where every horse bears his commanding rein,
And may direct his course as please himself,
As well the fear of harm as harm apparent,
In my opinion, ought to be prevented.

GLOU.   I hope the king made peace with all of us;
And the compact is firm and true in me.

RIV.   And so in me; and so, I think, in all:
Yet, since it is but green, it should be put
To no apparent likelihood of breach,
Which haply by much company might be urged:
Therefore I say with noble Buckingham,
That it is meet so few should fetch the prince.

HAST.   And so say I.

GLOU.   Then be it so; and go we to determine
Who they shall be that straight shall post to Ludlow.
Madam, and you, my mother, will you go
To give your censures[16] in this weighty business?

Q. ELIZ. ⎫
DUCH. ⎬ With all our hearts.

[*Exeunt all but* BUCKINGHAM *and* GLOUCESTER.]

BUCK.   My lord, whoever journeys to the prince,
For God's sake, let not us two stay behind;
For, by the way, I'll sort occasion,[17]
As index[18] to the story we late talk'd of,
To part the queen's proud kindred from the king.

GLOU.   My other self, my counsel's consistory,[19]
My oracle, my prophet! — My dear cousin,
I, like a child, will go by thy direction.
Towards Ludlow then, for we'll not stay behind.   [*Exeunt.*]

---

15. *the estate*] the state.
16. *censures*] opinions.
17. *sort occasion*] contrive an opportunity.
18. *index*] prelude, prologue. In early printed books, the index was placed in the preliminary pages.
19. *consistory*] a council or solemn assembly.

SCENE III. *London. A Street.*

Enter two Citizens, *meeting*

FIRST CIT.   Neighbour, well met: whither away so fast?
SEC. CIT.   I promise you, I scarcely know myself:
     Hear you the news abroad?
FIRST CIT.   Ay, that the king is dead.
SEC. CIT.   Bad news, by 'r lady, seldom comes the better:
     I fear, I fear, 'twill prove a troublous world.

Enter another Citizen

THIRD CIT.   Neighbours, God speed!
FIRST CIT.   Give you good morrow, sir.
THIRD CIT.   Doth this news hold of good King Edward's death?
SEC. CIT.   Ay, sir, it is too true; God help the while!
THIRD CIT.   Then, masters, look to see a troublous world.
FIRST CIT.   No, no; by God's good grace his son shall reign.
THIRD CIT.   Woe to that land that's govern'd by a child!
SEC. CIT.   In him there is a hope of government,
     That in his nonage council under him,
     And in his full and ripen'd years himself,
     No doubt, shall then and till then govern well.
FIRST CIT.   So stood the state when Henry the Sixth
     Was crown'd in Paris but at nine months old.
THIRD CIT.   Stood the state so? No, no, good friends, God wot;
     For then this land was famously enrich'd
     With politic grave counsel; then the king
     Had virtuous uncles to protect his grace.
FIRST CIT.   Why, so hath this, both by the father and mother.
THIRD CIT.   Better it were they all came by the father,
     Or by the father there were none at all;
     For emulation now, who shall be nearest,
     Will touch us all too near,[1] if God prevent not.
     O, full of danger is the Duke of Gloucester!
     And the queen's sons and brothers haught[2] and proud:
     And were they to be ruled, and not to rule,
     This sickly land might solace[3] as before.

---

1. *touch . . . near*] injure, hurt, hit.
2. *haught*] a common form of "haughty."
3. *solace*] find comfort, *not* give comfort.

FIRST CIT.   Come, come, we fear the worst; all shall be well.
THIRD CIT.   When clouds appear, wise men put on their cloaks;
    When great leaves fall, the winter is at hand;
    When the sun sets, who doth not look for night?
    Untimely storms make men expect a dearth.
    All may be well; but, if God sort[4] it so,
    'Tis more than we deserve, or I expect.
SEC. CIT.   Truly, the souls of men are full of dread:
    Ye cannot reason almost with a man
    That looks not heavily and full of fear.
THIRD CIT.   Before the times of change, still is it so:
    By a divine instinct men's minds mistrust
    Ensuing dangers; as, by proof, we see
    The waters swell before a boisterous storm.
    But leave it all to God. Whither away?
SEC. CIT.   Marry, we were sent for to the justices.
THIRD CIT.   And so was I: I'll bear you company.   [*Exeunt.*]

SCENE IV. *London. The Palace.*

Enter the ARCHBISHOP OF YORK, *the young* DUKE OF YORK, QUEEN ELIZABETH, *and the* DUCHESS OF YORK

ARCH.   Last night, I hear, they lay at Northampton;
    At Stony-Stratford will they be to-night:
    To-morrow, or next day, they will be here.
DUCH.   I long with all my heart to see the prince:
    I hope he is much grown since last I saw him.
Q. ELIZ.   But I hear, no; they say my son of York
    Hath almost overta'en him in his growth.
YORK.   Ay, mother; but I would not have it so.
DUCH.   Why, my young cousin, it is good to grow.
YORK.   Grandam, one night, as we did sit at supper,
    My uncle Rivers talk'd how I did grow
    More than my brother: "Ay," quoth my uncle Gloucester,
    "Small herbs have grace, great weeds do grow apace:"
    And since, methinks, I would not grow so fast,

---

4. *sort*] ordain.

Because sweet flowers are slow and weeds make haste.
DUCH.   Good faith, good faith, the saying did not hold
In him that did object the same to thee:
He was the wretched'st thing when he was young,
So long a-growing and so leisurely,
That, if this rule were true, he should be gracious.
ARCH.   Why, madam, so, no doubt, he is.
DUCH.   I hope so too; but yet let mothers doubt.
YORK.   Now, by my troth, if I had been remember'd,
I could have given my uncle's grace a flout,
To touch his growth nearer[1] than he touch'd mine.
DUCH.   How, my pretty York? I pray thee, let me hear it.
YORK.   Marry, they say my uncle grew so fast
That he could gnaw a crust at two hours old:
'Twas full two years ere I could get a tooth.
Grandam, this would have been a biting jest.
DUCH.   I pray thee, pretty York, who told thee this?
YORK.   Grandam, his nurse.
DUCH.   His nurse! why, she was dead ere thou wert born.
YORK.   If 'twere not she, I cannot tell who told me.
Q. ELIZ.   A parlous boy:[2] go to, you are too shrewd.
ARCH.   Good madam, be not angry with the child.
Q. ELIZ.   Pitchers have ears.

Enter a Messenger

ARCH.   Here comes a messenger. What news?
MESS.   Such news, my lord, as grieves me to unfold.
Q. ELIZ.   How fares the prince?
MESS.   Well, madam, and in health.
DUCH.   What is thy news then?
MESS.   Lord Rivers and Lord Grey are sent to Pomfret,
With them Sir Thomas Vaughan, prisoners.
DUCH.   Who hath committed them?
MESS.   The mighty dukes,
Gloucester and Buckingham.
Q. ELIZ.   For what offence?
MESS.   The sum of all I can, I have disclosed;
Why or for what these nobles were committed
Is all unknown to me, my gracious lady.
Q. ELIZ.   Ay me, I see the downfall of our house!
The tiger now hath seized the gentle hind;
Insulting tyranny begins to jet

---

1. *touch . . . nearer*] hit, in the slang sense of "get at."
2. *parlous boy*] an *enfant terrible*.

Upon the innocent and aweless throne:[3]
Welcome, destruction, death, and massacre!
I see, as in a map, the end of all.
DUCH.   Accursed and unquiet wrangling days,
How many of you have mine eyes beheld!
My husband lost his life to get the crown;
And often up and down my sons were toss'd,
For me to joy and weep their gain and loss:
And being seated, and domestic broils
Clean over-blown, themselves, the conquerors,
Make war upon themselves; blood against blood,
Self against self: O, preposterous
And frantic outrage, end thy damned spleen;
Or let me die, to look on death no more!
Q. ELIZ.   Come, come, my boy; we will to sanctuary.[4]
Madam, farewell.
DUCH.   I'll go along with you.
Q. ELIZ.   You have no cause.
ARCH.   My gracious lady, go;
And thither bear your treasure and your goods.
For my part, I'll resign unto your grace
The seal[5] I keep: and so betide to me
As well I tender you and all of yours!
Come, I'll conduct you to the sanctuary.   [*Exeunt.*]

ACT III.

SCENE I. *London. A Street.*

The trumpets sound. Enter the young PRINCE, *the Dukes of* GLOUCES-TER *and* BUCKINGHAM, CARDINAL BOURCHIER, CATESBY, *and others*

BUCK.   Welcome, sweet prince, to London, to your chamber.[1]

---

3. *to jet . . . throne*] to encroach upon a throne filled by an innocent child, and one inspiring no fear.
4. *sanctuary*] the precincts of Westminster Abbey, where no arrests of suspected persons were permitted.
5. *The seal*] the Great Seal of England.

---

1. *chamber*] London, the capital city of the kingdom, was formally called "camera regis" (king's chamber).

GLOU.   Welcome, dear cousin, my thoughts' sovereign:
     The weary way hath made you melancholy.
PRINCE.   No, uncle; but our crosses on the way
     Have made it tedious, wearisome, and heavy:
     I want more uncles here to welcome me.
GLOU.   Sweet prince, the untainted virtue of your years
     Hath not yet dived into the world's deceit:
     Nor more can you distinguish of a man
     Than of his outward show; which, God he knows,
     Seldom or never jumpeth with the heart.
     Those uncles which you want were dangerous;
     Your grace attended to their sugar'd words,
     But look'd not on the poison of their hearts:
     God keep you from them, and from such false friends!
PRINCE.   God keep me from false friends! but they were none.
GLOU.   My lord, the mayor of London comes to greet you.

Enter the Lord Mayor, *and his train*

MAY.   God bless your grace with health and happy days!
PRINCE.   I thank you, good my lord; and thank you all.
     I thought my mother and my brother York
     Would long ere this have met us on the way:
     Fie, what a slug is Hastings, that he comes not
     To tell us whether they will come or no!

Enter LORD HASTINGS

BUCK.   And, in good time here comes the sweating lord.
PRINCE.   Welcome, my lord: what, will our mother come?
HAST.   On what occasion, God he knows, not I,
     The queen your mother and your brother York
     Have taken sanctuary: the tender prince
     Would fain have come with me to meet your grace,
     But by his mother was perforce withheld.
BUCK.   Fie, what an indirect and peevish course
     Is this of hers! Lord cardinal, will your grace
     Persuade the queen to send the Duke of York
     Unto his princely brother presently?
     If she deny, Lord Hastings, go with him,
     And from her jealous arms pluck him perforce.
CARD.   My Lord of Buckingham, if my weak oratory
     Can from his mother win the Duke of York,
     Anon expect him here; but if she be obdurate
     To mild entreaties, God in heaven forbid

We should infringe the holy privilege
Of blessed sanctuary! not for all this land
Would I be guilty of so deep a sin.

BUCK. You are too senseless-obstinate,[2] my lord,
Too ceremonious and traditional:
Weigh it but with the grossness of this age,[3]
You break not sanctuary in seizing him.
The benefit thereof is always granted
To those whose dealings have deserved the place,
And those who have the wit to claim the place:
This prince hath neither claim'd it nor deserved it;
And therefore, in mine opinion, cannot have it:
Then, taking him from thence that is not there,
You break no privilege nor charter there.
Oft have I heard of sanctuary men;
But sanctuary children ne'er till now.

CARD. My lord, you shall o'er-rule my mind for once.
Come on, Lord Hastings, will you go with me?

HAST. I go, my lord.

PRINCE. Good lords, make all the speedy haste you may.
                         [*Exeunt* CARDINAL *and* HASTINGS.]
Say, uncle Gloucester, if our brother come,
Where shall we sojourn till our coronation?

GLOU. Where it seems best unto your royal self.
If I may counsel you, some day or two
Your highness shall repose you at the Tower:
Then where you please, and shall be thought most fit
For your best health and recreation.

PRINCE. I do not like the Tower, of any place.
Did Julius Cæsar build that place, my lord?

BUCK. He did, my gracious lord, begin that place;
Which, since, succeeding ages have re-edified.

PRINCE. Is it upon record, or else reported
Successively from age to age, he built it?

BUCK. Upon record, my gracious lord.

PRINCE. But say, my lord, it were not register'd,
Methinks the truth should live from age to age,
As 'twere retail'd[4] to all posterity,
Even to the general all-ending day.

GLOU. [*Aside*] So wise so young, they say, do never live long.

---

2. *senseless-obstinate*] unreasonable in obstinacy.
3. *Weigh . . . age*] Consider it in the light of the unlicensed temper of the times (which
calls for high-handed action).
4. *retail'd*] recounted, rehearsed.

PRINCE.   What say you, uncle?
GLOU.   I say, without characters,[5] fame lives long.
    [*Aside*] Thus, like the formal vice, Iniquity,[6]
    I moralize two meanings in one word.
PRINCE.   That Julius Cæsar was a famous man;
    With what his valour did enrich his wit,
    His wit set down to make his valour live:
    Death makes no conquest of this conqueror;
    For now he lives in fame, though not in life.
    I'll tell you what, my cousin Buckingham, —
BUCK.   What, my gracious lord?
PRINCE.   An if I live until I be a man,
    I'll win our ancient right in France again,
    Or die a soldier, as I lived a king.
GLOU.   [*Aside*] Short summers lightly[7] have a forward spring.

Enter young YORK, HASTINGS, *and the* CARDINAL

BUCK.   Now, in good time, here comes the Duke of York.
PRINCE.   Richard of York! how fares our loving brother?
YORK.   Well, my dread lord; so must I call you now.
PRINCE.   Ay, brother, to our grief, as it is yours:
    Too late[8] he died that might have kept that title,
    Which by his death hath lost much majesty.
GLOU.   How fares our cousin, noble Lord of York?
YORK.   I thank you, gentle uncle. O, my lord,
    You said that idle weeds are fast in growth:
    The prince my brother hath outgrown me far.
GLOU.   He hath, my lord.
YORK.   And therefore is he idle?
GLOU.   O, my fair cousin, I must not say so.
YORK.   Then he is more beholding to you than I.
GLOU.   He may command me as my sovereign;
    But you have power in me as in a kinsman.
YORK.   I pray you, uncle, give me this dagger.
GLOU.   My dagger, little cousin? with all my heart.
PRINCE.   A beggar, brother?

---

5. *without characters*] without the help of letters or inscriptions.
6. *Thus . . . Iniquity*] In the old Morality plays the leading character in attendance on the Devil bore the conventional ("formal") designation of "The Vice," and indulged in persistent word-play. The character was occasionally known by the more specific name of "Iniquity" or "Hypocrisy" or some other sin.
7. *lightly*] commonly; a rare usage deduced from the meaning of "easily" or "readily" which often attaches to the word.
8. *late*] lately, recently.

YORK.   Of my kind uncle, that I know will give;
    And being but a toy, which is no grief to give.
GLOU.   A greater gift than that I'll give my cousin.
YORK.   A greater gift! O, that's the sword to it.[9]
GLOU.   Ay, gentle cousin, were it light enough.
YORK.   O, then, I see, you will part but with light gifts;
    In weightier things you'll say a beggar nay.
GLOU.   It is too heavy for your grace to wear.
YORK.   I weigh it lightly,[10] were it heavier.
GLOU.   What, would you have my weapon, little lord?
YORK.   I would, that I might thank you as you call me.
GLOU.   How?
YORK.   Little.
PRINCE.   My Lord of York will still be cross[11] in talk:
    Uncle, your grace knows how to bear with him.
YORK.   You mean, to bear me, not to bear with me:
    Uncle, my brother mocks both you and me;
    Because that I am little, like an ape,
    He thinks that you should bear me on your shoulders.
BUCK.   With what a sharp-provided wit he reasons!
    To mitigate the scorn he gives his uncle,
    He prettily and aptly taunts himself:
    So cunning and so young is wonderful.
GLOU.   My lord, will 't please you pass along?
    Myself and my good cousin Buckingham
    Will to your mother, to entreat of her
    To meet you at the Tower and welcome you.
YORK.   What, will you go unto the Tower, my lord?
PRINCE.   My lord protector needs will have it so.
YORK.   I shall not sleep in quiet at the Tower.
GLOU.   Why, what should you fear?
YORK.   Marry, my uncle Clarence' angry ghost:
    My grandam told me he was murder'd there.
PRINCE.   I fear no uncles dead.
GLOU.   Nor none that live, I hope.
PRINCE.   An if they live, I hope I need not fear.
    But come, my lord; and with a heavy heart,
    Thinking on them, go I unto the Tower.
    [A *Sennet.*[12] *Exeunt all but* GLOUCESTER, BUCKINGHAM *and*
                                                CATESBY.

---

9. *the sword to it*] The belt, which carried the dagger, bore a sword in addition.
10. *I . . . lightly*] I should mind very little.
11. *cross*] at cross purposes, malapert.
12. *A Sennet*] a flourish on a trumpet, marking the entrance or exit of a procession.

BUCK.   Think you, my lord, this little prating York
         Was not incensed by his subtle mother
         To taunt and scorn you thus opprobriously?
GLOU.   No doubt, no doubt: O, 'tis a parlous boy;
         Bold, quick, ingenious, forward, capable:
         He is all the mother's, from the top to toe.
BUCK.   Well, let them rest. Come hither, Catesby.
         Thou art sworn as deeply to effect what we intend,
         As closely to conceal what we impart:
         Thou know'st our reasons urged upon the way;
         What think'st thou? is it not an easy matter
         To make William Lord Hastings of our mind,
         For the instalment of this noble duke
         In the seat royal of this famous isle?
CATE.   He for his father's sake so loves the prince,
         That he will not be won to aught against him.
BUCK.   What think'st thou then of Stanley? what will he?
CATE.   He will do all in all as Hastings doth.
BUCK.   Well, then, no more but this: go, gentle Catesby,
         And, as it were far off, sound thou Lord Hastings,
         How he doth stand affected[13] to our purpose;
         And summon him to-morrow to the Tower,
         To sit about the coronation.
         If thou dost find him tractable to us,
         Encourage him, and show him all our reasons:
         If he be leaden, icy-cold, unwilling,
         Be thou so too; and so break off your talk,
         And give us notice of his inclination:
         For we to-morrow hold divided councils,[14]
         Wherein thyself shalt highly be employ'd.
GLOU.   Commend me to Lord William: tell him, Catesby,
         His ancient knot of dangerous adversaries
         To-morrow are let blood[15] at Pomfret-castle;
         And bid my friend, for joy of this good news,
         Give Mistress Shore[16] one gentle kiss the more.
BUCK.   Good Catesby, go, effect this business soundly.
CATE.   My good lords both, with all the heed I may.
GLOU.   Shall we hear from you, Catesby, ere we sleep?
CATE.   You shall, my lord.

---

13. *stand affected*] feel disposed.
14. *divided councils*] two separate councils, one of Gloucester's supporters and the other of
    the young prince's.
15. *let blood*] killed, executed.
16. *Mistress Shore*] On Edward IV's death, according to Holinshed's *Chronicles*, Hastings
    made Jane Shore his mistress.

GLOU. At Crosby Place, there shall you find us both.

[*Exit* CATESBY.]

BUCK. Now, my lord, what shall we do, if we perceive
Lord Hastings will not yield to our complots?[17]

GLOU. Chop off his head, man; somewhat we will do:
And, look, when I am king, claim thou of me
The earldom of Hereford, and the moveables[18]
Whereof the king my brother stood possess'd.

BUCK. I'll claim that promise at your grace's hands.

GLOU. And look to have it yielded with all willingness.
Come, let us sup betimes, that afterwards
We may digest our complots in some form. [*Exeunt.*]

SCENE II. *Before Lord Hastings' House.*

Enter a Messenger

MESS. What, ho! my lord

HAST. [*Within*] Who knocks at the door?

MESS. A messenger from the Lord Stanley.

Enter LORD HASTINGS

HAST. What is 't o'clock?

MESS. Upon the stroke of four.

HAST. Cannot thy master sleep these tedious nights?

MESS. So it should seem by that I have to say.
First, he commends him to your noble lordship.

HAST. And then?

MESS. And then he sends you word
He dreamt to-night the boar had razed his helm:[1]
Besides, he says there are two councils held;
And that may be determined at the one
Which may make you and him to rue at the other.
Therefore he sends to know your lordship's pleasure,
If presently you will take horse with him,
And with all speed post with him toward the north,
To shun the danger that his soul divines.

---

17. *complots*] conspiracies.
18. *moveables*] any property, such as furniture, not fixed in place.

---

1. *razed his helm*] tore off his head. The boar refers to Gloucester.

HAST.   Go, fellow, go, return unto thy lord;
     Bid him not fear the separated councils:
     His honour and myself are at the one,
     And at the other is my servant Catesby;
     Where nothing can proceed that toucheth[2] us,
     Whereof I shall not have intelligence.
     Tell him his fears are shallow, wanting instance:[3]
     And for his dreams, I wonder he is so fond
     To trust the mockery of unquiet slumbers:
     To fly the boar before the boar pursues,
     Were to incense the boar to follow us,
     And make pursuit where he did mean no chase.
     Go, bid thy master rise and come to me;
     And we will both together to the Tower,
     Where, he shall see, the boar will use us kindly.
MESS.   My gracious lord, I'll tell him what you say.   [*Exit.*]

Enter CATESBY

CATE.   Many good morrows to my noble lord!
HAST.   Good morrow, Catesby; you are early stirring:
     What news, what news, in this our tottering state?
CATE.   It is a reeling world indeed, my lord;
     And I believe 'twill never stand upright
     Till Richard wear the garland of the realm.
HAST.   How! wear the garland! dost thou mean the crown?
CATE.   Ay, my good lord.
HAST.   I'll have this crown of mine cut from my shoulders,
     Ere I will see the crown so foul misplaced.
     But canst thou guess that he doth aim at it?
CATE.   Ay, on my life, and hopes to find you forward
     Upon his party for the gain thereof:
     And thereupon he sends you this good news,
     That this same very day your enemies,
     The kindred of the queen, must die at Pomfret.
HAST.   Indeed, I am no mourner for that news,
     Because they have been still[4] mine enemies:
     But, that I'll give my voice on Richard's side,
     To bar my master's heirs in true descent,
     God knows I will not do it, to the death.
CATE.   God keep your lordship in that gracious mind!

---

2. *toucheth*] injureth.
3. *wanting instance*] without example or proof.
4. *still*] always.

HAST.   But I shall laugh at this a twelve-month hence,
That they who brought me in my master's hate,
I live to look upon their tragedy.
I tell thee, Catesby, —
CATE.   What, my lord?
HAST.   Ere a fortnight make me elder,
I'll send some packing that yet think not on it.
CATE.   'Tis a vile thing to die, my gracious lord,
When men are unprepared and look not for it.
HAST.   O monstrous, monstrous! and so falls it out
With Rivers, Vaughan, Grey: and so 'twill do
With some men else, who think themselves as safe
As thou and I; who, as thou know'st, are dear
To princely Richard and to Buckingham.
CATE.   The princes both make high account of you;
[*Aside*] For they account his head upon the bridge.[5]
HAST.   I know they do; and I have well deserved it.

Enter LORD STANLEY

Come on, come on; where is your boar-spear, man?
Fear you the boar, and go so unprovided?
STAN.   My lord, good morrow; good morrow, Catesby:
You may jest on, but, by the holy rood,[6]
I do not like these several councils, I.
HAST.   My lord,
I hold my life as dear as you do yours;
And never in my life, I do protest,
Was it more precious to me than 'tis now:
Think you, but that I know our state secure,
I would be so triumphant as I am?
STAN.   The lords at Pomfret, when they rode from London,
Were jocund and supposed their state was sure,
And they indeed had no cause to mistrust;
But yet, you see, how soon the day o'ercast.
This sudden stab of rancour I misdoubt:
Pray God, I say, I prove a needless coward!
What, shall we toward the Tower? the day is spent.
HAST.   Come, come, have with you.[7] Wot[8] you what, my lord?
To-day the lords you talk of are beheaded.

---

5. *they account . . . bridge*] It was customary to put the heads of those who were executed for high treason on a pole fixed to the roof of a tower on London Bridge.
6. *rood*] the cross (on which Christ died).
7. *have with you*] I will go along with you.
8. *Wot*] know.

STAN.   They, for their truth, might better wear their heads,
      Than some that have accused them wear their hats.
      But come, my lord, let us away.

Enter a Pursuivant[9]

HAST.   Go on before; I'll talk with this good fellow.
                          [Exeunt STANLEY *and* CATESBY.]
      How now, sirrah! how goes the world with thee?
PURS.   The better that your lordship please to ask.
HAST.   I tell thee, man, 'tis better with me now,
      Than when I met thee last where now we meet:
      Then was I going prisoner to the Tower,
      By the suggestion of the queen's allies;
      But now, I tell thee — keep it to thyself —
      This day those enemies are put to death,
      And I in better state than e'er I was.
PURS.   God hold it,[10] to your honour's good content!
HAST.   Gramercy,[11] fellow: there, drink that for me.
                              [Throws him his purse.]
PURS.   God save your lordship.   *[Exit.]*

Enter a Priest

PRIEST.   Well met, my lord; I am glad to see your honour.
HAST.   I thank thee, good Sir John,[12] with all my heart.
      I am in your debt for your last exercise;[13]
      Come the next Sabbath, and I will content you.
                         [He whispers in his ear.]

Enter BUCKINGHAM

BUCK.   What, talking with a priest, lord chamberlain?
      Your friends at Pomfret, they do need the priest;
      Your honour hath no shriving work[14] in hand.
HAST.   Good faith, and when I met this holy man,
      Those men you talk of came into my mind.
      What, go you toward the Tower?
BUCK.   I do, my lord; but long I shall not stay:
      I shall return before your lordship thence.

---

  9. *Pursuivant*] Properly, an attendant on a herald, an officer of the college of arms, but the
     word was more often used, as here, for any messenger of a court of justice. It is also
     found in the general sense of messenger.
 10. *God hold it*] God continue your good fortune.
 11. *Gramercy*] great thanks.
 12. *good Sir John*] "Sir" was a courtesy title given to all clergymen.
 13. *exercise*] religious exhortation, sermon.
 14. *shriving work*] confession.

HAST.   'Tis like enough, for I stay dinner there.
BUCK.   [*Aside*] And supper too, although thou know'st it not.
Come, will you go?
HAST.   I'll wait upon your lordship.   [*Exeunt.*]

SCENE III. *Pomfret Castle.*

Enter SIR RICHARD RATCLIFF, *with halberds, carrying* RIVERS, GREY, *and* VAUGHAN *to death*

RAT.   Come, bring forth the prisoners.
RIV.   Sir Richard Ratcliff, let me tell thee this:
    To-day shalt thou behold a subject die
    For truth, for duty, and for loyalty.
GREY.   God keep the prince from all the pack of you!
    A knot you are of damned blood-suckers.
VAUG.   You live that shall cry woe for this hereafter.
RAT.   Dispatch; the limit of your lives is out.
RIV.   O Pomfret, Pomfret! O thou bloody prison,
    Fatal and ominous to noble peers!
    Within the guilty closure[1] of thy walls
    Richard the second here was hack'd to death;
    And, for more slander to thy dismal seat,
    We give thee up our guiltless blood to drink.
GREY.   Now Margaret's curse is fall'n upon our heads,
    For standing by when Richard stabb'd her son.
RIV.   Then cursed she Hastings, then cursed she Buckingham,
    Then cursed she Richard. O, remember, God,
    To hear her prayers for them, as now for us!
    And for my sister and her princely sons,
    Be satisfied, dear God, with our true blood,
    Which, as thou know'st, unjustly must be spilt.
RAT.   Make haste; the hour of death is expiate.[2]
RIV.   Come, Grey, come, Vaughan, let us all embrace:
    And take our leave, until we meet in heaven.   [*Exeunt.*]

---

1. *closure*] enclosure, compass.
2. *expiate*] brought to a close, finished.

SCENE IV. *The Tower of London.*

Enter BUCKINGHAM, DERBY, HASTINGS, *the* BISHOP OF ELY, RATCLIFF,
LOVEL, *with others, and take their seats at a table*

HAST.   My lords, at once: the cause why we are met
    Is, to determine of the coronation.
    In God's name, speak: when is the royal day?
BUCK.   Are all things fitting for that royal time?
DER.   It is, and wants but nomination.[1]
ELY.   To-morrow then I judge a happy day.
BUCK.   Who knows the lord protector's mind herein?
    Who is most inward[2] with the noble duke?
ELY.   Your grace, we think, should soonest know his mind.
BUCK.   Who, I, my lord! We know each other's faces,
    But for our hearts, he knows no more of mine
    Than I of yours;
    Nor I no more of his, than you of mine.
    Lord Hastings, you and he are near in love.
HAST.   I thank his grace, I know he loves me well;
    But, for his purpose in the coronation,
    I have not sounded him, nor he deliver'd
    His gracious pleasure any way therein:
    But you, my noble lords, may name the time;
    And in the duke's behalf I'll give my voice,
    Which, I presume, he'll take in gentle part.

Enter GLOUCESTER

ELY.   Now in good time, here comes the duke himself.
GLOU.   My noble lords and cousins all, good morrow.
    I have been long a sleeper; but, I hope,
    My absence doth neglect no great designs,
    Which by my presence might have been concluded.
BUCK.   Had not you come upon your cue, my lord,
    William Lord Hastings had pronounced your part, —
    I mean, your voice, — for crowning of the king.
GLOU.   Than my Lord Hastings no man might be bolder;
    His lordship knows me well, and loves me well.
HAST.   I thank your grace.

---

1. *nomination*] the naming of the day.
2. *inward*] intimate.

GLOU.   My Lord of Ely!
ELY.   My lord?
GLOU.   When I was last in Holborn,
    I saw good strawberries in your garden there:
    I do beseech you send for some of them.
ELY.   Marry, and will, my lord, with all my heart.   [*Exit.*]
GLOU.   Cousin of Buckingham, a word with you.
                                [*Drawing him aside.*]
    Catesby hath sounded Hastings in our business,
    And finds the testy gentleman so hot,
    As he will lose his head ere give consent
    His master's son, as worshipful he terms it,
    Shall lose the royalty of England's throne.
BUCK.   Withdraw you hence, my lord, I'll follow you.
              [*Exit* GLOUCESTER, BUCKINGHAM *following.*]
DER.   We have not yet set down this day of triumph.
    To-morrow, in mine opinion, is too sudden;
    For I myself am not so well provided
    As else I would be, were the day prolong'd.

Re-enter BISHOP OF ELY

ELY.   Where is my lord protector? I have sent for these strawberries.
HAST.   His grace looks cheerfully and smooth to-day;
    There's some conceit or other likes him[3] well,
    When he doth bid good morrow with such a spirit.
    I think there's never a man in Christendom
    That can less hide his love or hate than he;
    For by his face straight shall you know his heart.
DER.   What of his heart perceive you in his face
    By any likelihood he show'd to-day?
HAST.   Marry, that with no man here he is offended;
    For, were he, he had shown it in his looks.
DER.   I pray God he be not, I say.

Re-enter GLOUCESTER *and* BUCKINGHAM

GLOU.   I pray you all, tell me what they deserve
    That do conspire my death with devilish plots
    Of damned witchcraft, and that have prevail'd
    Upon my body with their hellish charms?
HAST.   The tender love I bear your grace, my lord,
    Makes me most forward in this noble presence

---

3. *some conceit . . . likes him*] Some thought or other pleases him.

To doom the offenders, whatsoever they be:
I say, my lord, they have deserved death.
GLOU.   Then be your eyes the witness of this ill:
See how I am bewitch'd; behold, mine arm
Is like a blasted sapling, withered up:
And this is Edward's wife, that monstrous witch,
Consorted with that harlot strumpet Shore,
That by their witchcraft thus have marked me.
HAST.   If they have done this thing, my gracious lord, —
GLOU.   If! thou protector of this damned strumpet,
Tellest thou me of "ifs"? Thou art a traitor:
Off with his head! Now, by Saint Paul I swear,
I will not dine until I see the same.
Lovel and Ratcliff, look that it be done:
The rest that love me, rise and follow me.
              [*Exeunt all but* HASTINGS, RATCLIFF *and* LOVEL.]
HAST.   Woe, woe for England! not a whit for me;
For I, too fond, might have prevented this.
Stanley did dream the boar did raze his helm;
But I disdain'd it, and did scorn to fly:
Three times to-day my foot-cloth horse did stumble,[4]
And startled, when he look'd upon the Tower,
As loath to bear me to the slaughter-house.
O, now I want the priest that spake to me:
I now repent I told the pursuivant,
As 'twere triumphing at mine enemies,
How they at Pomfret bloodily were butcher'd,
And I myself secure in grace and favour.
O Margaret, Margaret, now thy heavy curse
Is lighted on poor Hastings' wretched head!
RAT.   Dispatch, my lord; the duke would be at dinner:
Make a short shrift;[5] he longs to see your head.
HAST.   O momentary grace of mortal men,
Which we more hunt for than the grace of God!
Who builds his hopes in air of your fair looks,
Lives like a drunken sailor on a mast,
Ready, with every nod, to tumble down
Into the fatal bowels of the deep.
LOV.   Come, come, dispatch; 'tis bootless to exclaim.
HAST.   O bloody Richard! miserable England!
I prophesy the fearfull'st time to thee

---

4. *foot-cloth . . . stumble*] horse adorned with a rich cloth reaching nearly to the ground on
each side. It was considered an ill omen if one's horse stumbled.
5. *shrift*] confession.

That ever wretched age hath look'd upon.
Come, lead me to the block; bear him my head:
They smile at me that shortly shall be dead.   [*Exeunt.*]

SCENE V. *The Tower-Walls.*

Enter GLOUCESTER *and* BUCKINGHAM, *in rotten*[1] *armour, marvellous ill-favoured*

GLOU.   Come, cousin, canst thou quake, and change thy colour,
   Murder thy breath in middle of a word,
   And then begin again, and stop again,
   As if thou wert distraught and mad with terror?
BUCK.   Tut, I can counterfeit the deep tragedian,
   Speak and look back, and pry on every side,
   Tremble and start at wagging of a straw,
   Intending[2] deep suspicion: ghastly looks
   Are at my service, like enforced smiles;
   And both are ready in their offices,
   At any time, to grace my stratagems.
   But what, is Catesby gone?
GLOU.   He is; and, see, he brings the mayor along.

Enter the Mayor *and* CATESBY

BUCK.   Lord mayor, —
GLOU.   Look to the drawbridge there!
BUCK.   Hark! a drum.
GLOU.   Catesby, o'erlook the walls.
BUCK.   Lord mayor, the reason we have sent —
GLOU.   Look back, defend thee, here are enemies.
BUCK.   God and our innocency defend and guard us!
GLOU.   Be patient, they are friends, Ratcliff and Lovel.

Enter LOVEL *and* RATCLIFF, *with* HASTINGS' *head*

LOV.   Here is the head of that ignoble traitor,
   The dangerous and unsuspected Hastings.
GLOU.   So dear I loved the man, that I must weep.
   I took him for the plainest harmless creature

---

1. *rotten*] rusty.
2. *Intending*] pretending.

That breathed upon this earth a Christian;
Made him my book, wherein my soul recorded
The history of all her secret thoughts:
So smooth he daub'd his vice with show of virtue
That, his apparent open guilt omitted,[3]
I mean, his conversation[4] with Shore's wife,
He lived from all attainder of suspect.[5]

BUCK.   Well, well, he was the covert'st shelter'd traitor
That ever lived.
Would you imagine, or almost believe,
Were 't not that, by great preservation,
We live to tell it you, the subtle traitor
This day had plotted, in the council-house
To murder me and my good Lord of Gloucester?

MAY.   What, had he so?

GLOU.   What, think you we are Turks or infidels?
Or that we would, against the form of law,
Proceed thus rashly to the villain's death,
But that the extreme peril of the case,
The peace of England and our persons' safety,
Enforced us to this execution?

MAY.   Now, fair befall you![6] he deserved his death;
And you, my good lords both, have well proceeded,
To warn false traitors from the like attempts.
I never look'd for better at his hands,
After he once fell in with Mistress Shore.

GLOU.   Yet had not we determined he should die,
Until your lordship came to see his death;
Which now the loving haste of these our friends,
Somewhat against our meaning, have prevented:
Because, my lord, we would have had you heard
The traitor speak and timorously confess
The manner and the purpose of his treason;
That you might well have signified the same
Unto the citizens, who haply may
Misconstrue us in him and wail his death.

MAY.   But, my good lord, your grace's word shall serve,
As well as I had seen and heard him speak:
And doubt you not, right noble princes both,
But I'll acquaint our duteous citizens

3. *apparent . . . omitted*] manifest . . . excepted.
4. *conversation*] criminal conversation.
5. *from all attainder of suspect*] free from all taint of suspicion.
6. *fair befall you!*] Good fortune attend you!

With all your just proceedings in this cause.
GLOU.   And to that end we wish'd your lordship here,
To avoid the carping censures of the world.
BUCK.   But since you come too late of our intents,[7]
Yet witness what you hear we did intend:
And so, my good lord mayor, we bid farewell.   [*Exit* Mayor.]
GLOU.   Go, after, after, cousin Buckingham.
The mayor towards Guildhall hies him in all post:
There, at your meet'st advantage[8] of the time,
Infer[9] the bastardy of Edward's children:
Tell them how Edward put to death a citizen,
Only for saying he would make his son
Heir to the crown, meaning indeed his house,
Which, by the sign thereof, was termed so.[10]
Moreover, urge his hateful luxury
And bestial appetite in change of lust;[11]
Which stretched to their servants, daughters, wives,
Even where his lustful eye or savage heart,
Without control, listed to make his prey.
Nay, for a need, thus far come near my person:
Tell them, when that my mother went with child
Of that unsatiate Edward, noble York,
My princely father, then had wars in France;
And, by just computation of the time,
Found that the issue was not his begot;
Which well appeared in his lineaments,
Being nothing like the noble duke my father:
But touch this sparingly, as 'twere far off;
Because you know, my lord, my mother lives.
BUCK.   Fear not, my lord, I'll play the orator,
As if the golden fee for which I plead
Were for myself: and so, my lord, adieu.
GLOU.   If you thrive well, bring them to Baynard's Castle;[12]

---

7. *too late of our intents*] too late for our plans or purposes.
8. *meet'st advantage*] fittest opportunity.
9. *Infer*] allege, suggest.
10. *a citizen . . . termed so*] The historian Edward Hall (c. 1498–1547) describes the execution by Edward IV's order, on the grounds given in these lines, of a citizen named Burdet, "who dwelt in Cheap Side, *at the signe of the Croune,* . . . over against Soper Lane."
11. *in change of lust*] driven by a constant desire for new mistresses.
12. *Baynard's Castle*] a palatial residence in the city of London, on the north bank of the Thames, not far from the south side of St. Paul's Cathedral. It had been recently occupied by Gloucester's father, Richard, Duke of York.

Where you shall find me well accompanied
With reverend fathers and well-learned bishops.
BUCK.   I go; and towards three or four o'clock
Look for the news that the Guildhall affords.   [*Exit.*]
GLOU.   Go, Lovel, with all speed to Doctor Shaw;
[*To Cate.*] Go thou to Friar Penker;[13] bid them both
Meet me within this hour at Baynard's Castle.
                              [*Exeunt all but* GLOUCESTER.]
Now will I in, to take some privy order,
To draw the brats of Clarence out of sight;
And to give notice, that no manner of person
At any time have recourse unto the princes.   [*Exit.*]

SCENE VI. *The Same. A Street.*

Enter a Scrivener, *with a paper in his hand*

SCRIV.   This is the indictment of the good Lord Hastings;
Which in a set hand fairly is engross'd,
That it may be this day read o'er in Paul's.
And mark how well the sequel hangs together:
Eleven hours I spent to write it over,
For yesternight by Catesby was it brought me;
The precedent[1] was full as long a-doing:
And yet within these five hours lived Lord Hastings,
Untainted, unexamined, free, at liberty.
Here's a good world the while! Why, who's so gross,
That seeth not this palpable device?
Yet who's so blind, but says he sees it not?
Bad is the world; and all will come to nought,
When such bad dealing must be seen in thought.[2]   [*Exit.*]

---

13. *Doctor Shaw . . . Friar Penker*] well-known preachers of the day. Doctor Shaw was
      brother of the Lord Mayor.

---

  1. *precedent*] first draft.
  2. *in thought*] in silence, unvoiced.

SCENE VII. *Baynard's Castle.*

Enter GLOUCESTER *and* BUCKINGHAM, *at several doors*

GLOU.　How now, my lord, what say the citizens?

BUCK.　Now, by the holy mother of our Lord,
　　The citizens are mum, and speak not a word.

GLOU.　Touch'd you the bastardy of Edward's children?

BUCK.　I did; with his contract with Lady Lucy,
　　And his contract by deputy in France;[1]
　　The insatiate greediness of his desires,
　　And his enforcement of the city wives;
　　His tyranny for trifles; his own bastardy,
　　As being got, your father then in France,
　　And his resemblance, being not like the duke:
　　Withal I did infer your lineaments,
　　Being the right idea of your father,
　　Both in your form and nobleness of mind;
　　Laid open all your victories in Scotland,
　　Your discipline in war, wisdom in peace,
　　Your bounty, virtue, fair humility;
　　Indeed left nothing fitting for the purpose
　　Untouch'd or slightly handled in discourse:
　　And when mine oratory grew to an end,
　　I bid them that did love their country's good
　　Cry "God save Richard, England's royal king!"

GLOU.　Ah! and did they so?

BUCK.　No, so God help me, they spake not a word;
　　But, like dumb statuës[2] or breathing stones,
　　Gazed each on other, and look'd deadly pale.
　　Which when I saw, I reprehended them;
　　And ask'd the mayor what meant this wilful silence:
　　His answer was, the people were not wont
　　To be spoke to but by the recorder.
　　Then he was urged to tell my tale again:
　　"Thus saith the duke, thus hath the duke inferr'd;"

1. *contract . . . France*] It was said that Edward was contracted to marry a woman named Elizabeth Lucy before his marriage to Lady Elizabeth Grey; a proposal that Edward IV should marry Lady Bona, the sister of King Louis XI of France, was made by the Earl of Warwick, acting as the king's deputy, but did not get beyond the stage of discussion.
2. *statuës*] This word is always a trisyllable in Shakespeare, and is often written "statuas."

But nothing spake in warrant from himself.
When he had done, some followers of mine own
At the lower end of the hall hurl'd up their caps,
And some ten voices cried "God save King Richard!"
And thus I took the vantage of those few,
"Thanks, gentle citizens and friends!" quoth I,
"This general applause and loving shout
Argues your wisdoms and your love to Richard;"
And even here brake off, and came away.

GLOU.   What tongueless blocks were they! would they not speak?
BUCK.   No, by my troth, my lord.
GLOU.   Will not the mayor then and his brethren come?
BUCK.   The mayor is here at hand: intend[3] some fear;
Be not you spoke with, but by mighty suit:
And look you get a prayer-book in your hand,
And stand betwixt two churchmen, good my lord;
For on that ground I'll build a holy descant:[4]
And be not easily won to our request;
Play the maid's part, still answer nay, and take it.
GLOU.   I go; and if you plead as well for them
As I can say nay to thee for myself,
No doubt we'll bring it to a happy issue.
BUCK.   Go, go up to the leads;[5] the lord mayor knocks.

[*Exit* GLOUCESTER.]

Enter the Mayor *and* Citizens

Welcome, my lord: I dance attendance here;
I think the duke will not be spoke withal.

Enter CATESBY

Here comes his servant: how now, Catesby,
What says he?
CATE.   My lord, he doth entreat your grace
To visit him to-morrow or next day:
He is within, with two right reverend fathers,
Divinely bent to meditation;
And in no worldly suit would he be moved,
To draw him from his holy exercise.
BUCK.   Return, good Catesby, to thy lord again;

---

3. *intend*] pretend.
4. *ground . . . descant*] "Ground" is the core melody to which "descant" is added as an accompaniment, usually in a higher voice.
5. *the leads*] the roof, the topmost part of the building, which was covered with sheets of lead.

    Tell him, myself, the mayor and citizens,
    In deep designs and matters of great moment,
    No less importing than our general good,
    Are come to have some conference with his grace.
CATE.   I'll tell him what you say, my lord.   [*Exit.*]
BUCK.   Ah, ha, my lord, this prince is not an Edward!
    He is not lolling on a lewd day-bed,
    But on his knees at meditation;
    Not dallying with a brace of courtezans,
    But meditating with two deep divines;
    Not sleeping, to engross[6] his idle body,
    But praying, to enrich his watchful soul:
    Happy were England, would this gracious prince
    Take on himself the sovereignty thereof:
    But, sure, I fear, we shall ne'er win him to it.
MAY.   Marry, God forbid his grace should say us nay!
BUCK.   I fear he will.

Re-enter CATESBY

    How now, Catesby, what says your lord?
CATE.   My lord,
    He wonders to what end you have assembled
    Such troops of citizens to speak with him,
    His grace not being warn'd thereof before:
    My lord, he fears you mean no good to him.
BUCK.   Sorry I am my noble cousin should
    Suspect me, that I mean no good to him:
    By heaven, I come in perfect love to him;
    And so once more return and tell his grace.   [*Exit* CATESBY.]
    When holy and devout religious men
    Are at their beads, 'tis hard to draw them thence,
    So sweet is zealous contemplation.

Enter GLOUCESTER *aloft, between two* Bishops. CATESBY *returns*

MAY.   See, where he stands between two clergymen!
BUCK.   Two props of virtue for a Christian prince,
    To stay him from the fall of vanity:
    And, see, a book of prayer in his hand,
    True ornaments to know a holy man.
    Famous Plantagenet, most gracious prince,
    Lend favourable ears to our request;
    And pardon us the interruption
    Of thy devotion and right Christian zeal.

---

6. *engross*] make gross, fatten.

GLOU.   My lord, there needs no such apology:
     I rather do beseech you pardon me,
     Who, earnest in the service of my God,
     Neglect the visitation of my friends.
     But, leaving this, what is your grace's pleasure?
BUCK.   Even that, I hope, which pleaseth God above,
     And all good men of this ungovern'd isle.
GLOU.   I do suspect I have done some offence
     That seems disgracious in the city's eyes,
     And that you come to reprehend my ignorance.
BUCK.   You have, my lord: would it might please your grace,
     At our entreaties, to amend that fault!
GLOU.   Else wherefore breathe I in a Christian land?
BUCK.   Then know, it is your fault that you resign
     The supreme seat, the throne majestical,
     The scepter'd office of your ancestors,
     Your state of fortune and your due of birth,
     The lineal glory of your royal house,
     To the corruption of a blemish'd stock:
     Whilst, in the mildness of your sleepy thoughts,
     Which here we waken to our country's good,
     This noble isle doth want her proper limbs;
     Her face defaced with scars of infamy,
     Her royal stock graft with ignoble plants,
     And almost shoulder'd in[7] the swallowing gulf
     Of blind forgetfulness and dark oblivion.
     Which to recure,[8] we heartily solicit
     Your gracious self to take on you the charge
     And kingly government of this your land;
     Not as protector, steward, substitute,
     Or lowly factor for another's gain;
     But as successively,[9] from blood to blood,
     Your right of birth, your empery,[10] your own.
     For this, consorted with the citizens,
     Your very worshipful and loving friends,
     And by their vehement instigation,
     In this just suit come I to move your grace.
GLOU.   I know not whether to depart in silence,
     Or bitterly to speak in your reproof,
     Best fitteth my degree or your condition:

_____

   7. *shoulder'd in*] jostled into.
   8. *recure*] cure.
   9. *successively*] in due succession.
  10. *empery*] dominion.

If not to answer, you might haply think
Tongue-tied ambition, not replying, yielded
To bear the golden yoke of sovereignty,
Which fondly you would here impose on me;
If to reprove you for this suit of yours
So season'd with your faithful love to me,
Then, on the other side, I check'd my friends.
Therefore, to speak, and to avoid the first,
And then, in speaking, not to incur the last,
Definitively thus I answer you.
Your love deserves my thanks, but my desert
Unmeritable shuns your high request.
First, if all obstacles were cut away
And that my path were even to the crown,
As my right revenue and due by birth;
Yet so much is my poverty of spirit,
So mighty and so many my defects,
As I had rather hide me from my greatness,
Being a bark[11] to brook no mighty sea,
Than in my greatness covet to be hid,
And in the vapour of my glory smother'd.
But, God be thanked, there's no need of me,
And much I need to help you,[12] if need were;
The royal tree hath left us royal fruit,
Which, mellow'd by the stealing hours of time,
Will well become the seat of majesty,
And make, no doubt, us happy by his reign.
On him I lay what you would lay on me,
The right and fortune of his happy stars;
Which God defend that I should wring from him!
BUCK.   My lord, this argues conscience in your grace;
But the respects thereof are nice[13] and trivial,
All circumstances well considered.
You say that Edward is your brother's son:
So say we too, but not by Edward's wife;
For first he was contract[14] to Lady Lucy —
Your mother lives a witness to that vow —
And afterward by substitute betroth'd
To Bona, sister to the King of France.
These both put by, a poor petitioner,

11. *bark*] a boat propelled by oars or sails.
12. *need*] lack (the capacity to help you).
13. *nice*] punctilious, fanciful.
14. *contract*] betrothed.

A care-crazed mother of a many children,
A beauty-waning and distressed widow,
Even in the afternoon of her best days,
Made prize and purchase of his lustful eye,
Seduced the pitch[15] and height of all his thoughts
To base declension and loathed bigamy:[16]
By her, in his unlawful bed, he got[17]
This Edward, whom our manners term the prince.
More bitterly could I expostulate,
Save that, for reverence to some alive,
I give a sparing limit to my tongue.
Then, good my lord, take to your royal self
This proffer'd benefit of dignity;
If not to bless us and the land withal,
Yet to draw forth your noble ancestry
From the corruption of abusing times,
Unto a lineal true-derived course.

MAY.   Do, good my lord, your citizens entreat you.

BUCK.   Refuse not, mighty lord, this proffer'd love.

CATE.   O, make them joyful, grant their lawful suit!

GLOU.   Alas, why would you heap these cares on me?
I am unfit for state and majesty:
I do beseech you, take it not amiss;
I cannot nor I will not yield to you.

BUCK.   If you refuse it, — as, in love and zeal,
Loath to depose the child, your brother's son;
As well we know your tenderness of heart
And gentle, kind, effeminate remorse,[18]
Which we have noted in you to your kin,
And egally[19] indeed to all estates, —
Yet whether you accept our suit or no,
Your brother's son shall never reign our king;
But we will plant some other in the throne,
To the disgrace and downfall of your house:
And in this resolution here we leave you.
Come, citizens: 'zounds![20] I'll entreat no more.

---

15. *pitch*] a common term in falconry for the hawk's highest flight.
16. *bigamy*] According to canon law in Edward IV's time, marriage with a widow constituted bigamy.
17. *got*] begot, sired.
18. *remorse*] sense of pity.
19. *egally*] equally.
20. *'zounds*] an oath contracted from "God's wounds!", a reference to the wounds Christ received at his trial and on the Cross.

GLOU. O, do not swear, my lord of Buckingham.

[*Exit* BUCKINGHAM *with the* Citizens.]

CATE. Call them again, my lord, and accept their suit:

ANOTHER. Do, good my lord, lest all the land do rue it.

GLOU. Would you enforce me to a world of care?
    Well, call them again. I am not made of stones,
    But penetrable to your kind entreats,
    Albeit against my conscience and my soul.

Re-enter BUCKINGHAM *and the rest*

    Cousin of Buckingham, and you sage, grave men,
    Since you will buckle fortune on my back,
    To bear her burthen, whether I will or no,
    I must have patience to endure the load:
    But if black scandal or foul-faced reproach
    Attend the sequel of your imposition,
    Your mere enforcement shall acquittance[21] me
    From all the impure blots and stains thereof;
    For God he knows, and you may partly see,
    How far I am from the desire thereof.

MAY. God bless your grace! we see it, and will say it.

GLOU. In saying so, you shall but say the truth.

BUCK. Then I salute you with this kingly title:
    Long live Richard, England's royal king!

MAY. AND CIT. Amen.

BUCK. To-morrow will it please you to be crown'd?

GLOU. Even when you please, since you will have it so.

BUCK. To-morrow then we will attend your grace:
    And so most joyfully we take our leave.

GLOU. Come, let us to our holy task again.
    Farewell, good cousin; farewell, gentle friends.   [*Exeunt.*]

---

21. *acquittance*] acquit.

ACT IV.

SCENE I. *Before the Tower.*

Enter, on one side, QUEEN ELIZABETH, DUCHESS OF YORK, *and* MAR-
QUESS OF DORSET; *on the other,* ANNE, DUCHESS OF GLOUCESTER,
leading LADY MARGARET PLANTAGENET, CLARENCE'S *young daughter*

DUCH.   Who meets us here? my niece[1] Plantagenet
    Led in the hand of her kind aunt Gloucester?[2]
    Now, for my life, she's wandering to the Tower,
    On pure heart's love to greet the tender princes.
    Daughter, well met.
ANNE.   God give your graces both
    A happy and a joyful time of day!
Q. ELIZ.   As much to you, good sister! Whither away?
ANNE.   No farther than the Tower, and, as I guess,
    Upon the like devotion as yourselves,
    To gratulate the gentle princes there.
Q. ELIZ.   Kind sister, thanks: we'll enter all together.

Enter BRAKENBURY

    And, in good time, here the lieutenant comes.
    Master lieutenant, pray you, by your leave,
    How doth the prince, and my young son of York?
BRAK.   Right well, dear madam. By your patience,
    I may not suffer you to visit them;
    The king hath straitly charged the contrary.
Q. ELIZ.   The king! why, who's that?
BRAK.   I cry you mercy: I mean the lord protector.
Q. ELIZ.   The Lord protect him from that kingly title!
    Hath he set bounds betwixt their love and me?
    I am their mother; who should keep me from them?
DUCH.   I am their father's mother; I will see them.
ANNE.   Their aunt I am in law,[3] in love their mother:

---

1. *niece*] granddaughter.
2. *aunt Gloucester*] Anne, widow, or rather affianced bride, of Prince Edward, Henry VI's
   son and heir, was solicited in marriage by Gloucester while acting as chief mourner at
   Henry VI's funeral and is now married to him. Lady Margaret Plantagenet, whom she
   holds by the hand, was daughter of her sister, the late Duchess of Clarence.
3. *in law*] by marriage.

Then bring me to their sights; I'll bear thy blame,
And take thy office from thee, on my peril.
BRAK.　No, madam, no; I may not leave it[4] so:
I am bound by oath, and therefore pardon me.　　　[*Exit.*]

Enter LORD STANLEY

STAN.　Let me but meet you, ladies, one hour hence,
And I'll salute your grace of York as mother,
And reverend looker on, of two fair queens.
[*To Anne.*] Come, madam, you must straight to Westminster,
There to be crowned Richard's royal queen.
Q. ELIZ.　O, cut my lace in sunder, that my pent heart
May have some scope to beat, or else I swoon
With this dead-killing news!
ANNE.　Despiteful tidings! O unpleasing news!
DOR.　Be of good cheer: mother, how fares your grace?
Q. ELIZ.　O Dorset, speak not to me, get thee hence!
Death and destruction dog thee at the heels;
Thy mother's name is ominous to children.
If thou wilt outstrip death, go cross the seas,
And live with Richmond,[5] from the reach of hell:
Go, hie thee, hie thee from this slaughter-house,
Lest thou increase the number of the dead;
And make me die the thrall of Margaret's curse,
Nor mother, wife, nor England's counted queen.
STAN.　Full of wise care is this your counsel, madam.
Take all the swift advantage of the hours;
You shall have letters from me to my son
To meet you on the way, and welcome you.
Be not ta'en tardy by unwise delay.
DUCH.　O ill-dispersing wind of misery!
O my accursed womb, the bed of death!
A cockatrice[6] hast thou hatch'd to the world,
Whose unavoided eye is murderous.
STAN.　Come, madam, come; I in all haste was sent.
ANNE.　And I in all unwillingness will go.
I would to God that the inclusive verge
Of golden metal that must round my brow

---

4. *leave it*] part from my office, infringe my duty.
5. *cross . . . Richmond*] Henry Tudor, Earl of Richmond (later Henry VII) and head of the
House of Lancaster after Henry VI's death, was in Brittany at the time.
6. *cockatrice*] a fabulous serpent, also known as the basilisk, whose glance was deadly.

Were red-hot steel,[7] to sear me to the brain!
Anointed let me be with deadly venom,
And die, ere men can say, God save the queen!
Q. ELIZ.   Go, go, poor soul, I envy not thy glory;
    To feed my humour, wish thyself no harm.
ANNE.   No! why? When he that is my husband now
    Came to me, as I follow'd Henry's corse,
    When scarce the blood was well wash'd from his hands
    Which issued from my other angel husband,
    And that dead saint which then I weeping follow'd;
    O, when, I say, I look'd on Richard's face,
    This was my wish: "Be thou," quoth I, "accursed,
    For making me, so young, so old a widow!
    And, when thou wed'st, let sorrow haunt thy bed;
    And be thy wife — if any be so mad —
    As miserable by the death of thee
    As thou hast made me by my dear lord's death!"
    Lo, ere I can repeat this curse again,
    Even in so short a space, my woman's heart
    Grossly grew captive to his honey words,
    And proved the subject of my own soul's curse,
    Which ever since hath kept my eyes from rest;
    For never yet one hour in his bed
    Have I enjoy'd the golden dew of sleep,
    But have been waked by his timorous dreams.
    Besides, he hates me for my father Warwick;
    And will, no doubt, shortly be rid of me.
Q. ELIZ.   Poor heart, adieu! I pity thy complaining.
ANNE.   No more than from my soul I mourn for yours.
DOR.   Farewell, thou woful welcomer of glory!
ANNE.   Adieu, poor soul, that takest thy leave of it!
DUCH.   [To DORSET] Go thou to Richmond, and good fortune guide
    thee!
    [To ANNE] Go thou to Richard, and good angels guard thee!
    [To QUEEN ELIZ.] Go thou to sanctuary, and good thoughts possess
    thee!
    I to my grave, where peace and rest lie with me!
    Eighty odd years of sorrow have I seen,
    And each hour's joy wreck'd with a week of teen.[8]
Q. ELIZ.   Stay, yet look back with me unto the Tower.

---

7. *red-hot steel*] Regicides or conspirators against the lives of kings were often punished in
    the middle ages by setting on their brows a crown of iron heated red-hot.
8. *teen*] grief.

Pity, you ancient stones, those tender babes
Whom envy hath immured within your walls!
Rough cradle for such little pretty ones!
Rude ragged nurse, old sullen playfellow
For tender princes, use my babies well!
So foolish sorrow bids your stones farewell.   [*Exeunt.*]

SCENE II. *London. The Palace.*

Sennet. Enter RICHARD, *in pomp, crowned;* BUCKINGHAM, CATESBY, *a* Page, *and others*

K. RICH.   Stand all apart. Cousin of Buckingham!
BUCK.   My gracious sovereign?
K. RICH.   Give me thy hand. [*Here he ascendeth the throne.*] Thus
    high, by thy advice
    And thy assistance, is king Richard seated:
    But shall we wear these honours for a day?
    Or shall they last, and we rejoice in them?
BUCK.   Still live they, and for ever may they last!
K. RICH.   O Buckingham, now do I play the touch,[1]
    To try if thou be current gold indeed:
    Young Edward lives: think now what I would say.
BUCK.   Say on, my loving lord.
K. RICH.   Why, Buckingham, I say, I would be king.
BUCK.   Why, so you are, my thrice renowned liege.
K. RICH.   Ha! am I king? 'tis so: but Edward lives.
BUCK.   True, noble prince.
K. RICH.   O bitter consequence,
    That Edward still should live true noble prince!
    Cousin, thou wert not wont to be so dull:
    Shall I be plain? I wish the bastards dead;
    And I would have it suddenly perform'd.
    What sayest thou? speak suddenly; be brief.
BUCK.   Your grace may do your pleasure.
K. RICH.   Tut, tut, thou art all ice, thy kindness freezeth:
    Say, have I thy consent that they shall die?
BUCK.   Give me some breath, some little pause, my lord,
    Before I positively speak herein:

---

1. *play the touch*] make play with the touchstone, or true test (of metals).

I will resolve[2] your grace immediately.   [*Exit.*]
CATE.   [*Aside to a stander by*] The king is angry: see, he bites the lip.
K. RICH.   I will converse with iron-witted[3] fools
            And unrespective[4] boys: none are for me
            That look into me with considerate eyes:
            High-reaching Buckingham grows circumspect.
            Boy!
PAGE.   My lord?
K. RICH.   Know'st thou not any whom corrupting gold
            Would tempt unto a close exploit of death?
PAGE.   My lord, I know a discontented gentleman,
            Whose humble means match not his haughty mind:
            Gold were as good as twenty orators,
            And will, no doubt, tempt him to any thing.
K. RICH.   What is his name?
PAGE.   His name, my lord, is Tyrrel.
K. RICH.   I partly know the man: go, call him hither.   [*Exit* Page.]
            The deep-revolving witty[5] Buckingham
            No more shall be the neighbour to my counsel:
            Hath he so long held out with me untired,
            And stops he now for breath?

Enter STANLEY

            How now! what news with you?
STAN.   My lord, I hear the Marquis Dorset's fled
            To Richmond, in those parts beyond the seas
            Where he abides.   [*Stands apart.*]
K. RICH.   Catesby!
CATE.   My lord?
K. RICH.   Rumour it abroad
            That Anne, my wife, is sick and like to die:
            I will take order[6] for her keeping close.
            Inquire me out some mean-born gentleman,
            Whom I will marry straight to Clarence' daughter:
            The boy is foolish, and I fear not him.
            Look, how thou dream'st! I say again, give out
            That Anne my wife is sick, and like to die:
            About it; for it stands me much upon,[7]

---

2. *resolve*] definitely answer, satisfy.
3. *iron-witted*] dull-witted, wooden-headed.
4. *unrespective*] careless, thoughtless.
5. *witty*] knowing, clever.
6. *take order*] take measures, arrange.
7. *it stands me much upon*] It is a matter of importance for me.

To stop all hopes whose growth may damage me.

[*Exit* CATESBY.]

I must be married to my brother's daughter,[8]
Or else my kingdom stands on brittle glass.
Murder her brothers, and then marry her!
Uncertain way of gain! But I am in
So far in blood that sin will pluck on[9] sin:
Tear-falling pity dwells not in this eye.

Re-enter Page, *with* TYRREL

Is thy name Tyrrel?
TYR.   James Tyrrel, and your most obedient subject.
K. RICH.   Art thou, indeed?
TYR.   Prove me, my gracious sovereign.
K. RICH.   Darest thou resolve to kill a friend of mine?
TYR.   Ay, my lord;
But I had rather kill two enemies.
K. RICH.   Why, there thou hast it: two deep enemies,
Foes to my rest and my sweet sleep's disturbers
Are they that I would have thee deal upon:[10]
Tyrrel, I mean those bastards in the Tower.
TYR.   Let me have open means to come to them,
And soon I'll rid you from the fear of them.
K. RICH.   Thou sing'st sweet music. Hark, come hither, Tyrrel:
Go, by this token: rise, and lend thine ear: [*Whispers.*]
There is no more but so: say it is done,
And I will love thee, and prefer thee too.
TYR.   'Tis done, my gracious lord.
K. RICH.   Shall we hear from thee, Tyrrel, ere we sleep?
TYR.   Ye shall, my lord.   [*Exit.*]

Re-enter BUCKINGHAM

BUCK.   My lord, I have consider'd in my mind
The late demand that you did sound me in.
K. RICH.   Well, let that pass. Dorset is fled to Richmond.
BUCK.   I hear that news, my lord.
K. RICH.   Stanley, he is your wife's son:[11] well, look to it.
BUCK.   My lord, I claim your gift, my due by promise,
For which your honour and your faith is pawn'd;

---

8. *my brother's daughter*] Edward IV's eldest daughter Elizabeth, who happily escaped
marriage with her uncle and became the wife of his successor Henry VII.
9. *pluck on*] excite, cause.
10. *deal upon*] deal with.
11. *Stanley . . . son*] Stanley was married to Margaret Beaufort, the widow of Edmund
Tudor, Richmond's father.

The earldom of Hereford and the moveables
The which you promised I should possess.
K. RICH.   Stanley, look to your wife: if she convey
Letters to Richmond, you shall answer it.
BUCK.   What says your highness to my just demand?
K. RICH.   As I remember, Henry the Sixth
Did prophesy that Richmond should be king,
When Richmond was a little peevish boy.
A king, perhaps, perhaps, —
BUCK.   My lord!
K. RICH.   How chance the prophet could not at that time
Have told me, I being by, that I should kill him?
BUCK.   My lord, your promise for the earldom, —
K. RICH.   Richmond! When last I was at Exeter,
The mayor in courtesy show'd me the castle,
And call'd it Rougemont: at which name I started,
Because a bard of Ireland told me once,
I should not live long after I saw Richmond.
BUCK.   My lord!
K. RICH.   Ay, what's o'clock?
BUCK.   I am thus bold to put your grace in mind
Of what you promised me.
K. RICH.   Well, but what's o'clock?
BUCK.   Upon the stroke of ten.
K. RICH.   Well, let it strike.
BUCK.   Why let it strike?
K. RICH.   Because that, like a Jack,[12] thou keep'st the stroke
Betwixt thy begging and my meditation.
I am not in the giving vein to-day.
BUCK.   Why, then resolve me whether you will or no.
K. RICH.   Tut, tut,
Thou troublest me; I am not in the vein.
                                        [*Exeunt all but* BUCKINGHAM.]
BUCK.   Is it even so? rewards he my true service
With such deep contempt? made I him king for this?
O, let me think on Hastings, and be gone
To Brecknock,[13] while my fearful[14] head is on!   [*Exit.*]

---

12. *a Jack*] a small mechanical figure that struck the hour on the bell of a clock.
13. *Brecknock*] Brecknock Castle, in South Wales, was one of the Duke of Buckingham's residences.
14. *fearful*] full of fear.

SCENE III. *The Same.*

Enter TYRREL

TYR.   The tyrannous and bloody deed is done,
The most arch[1] act of piteous massacre
That ever yet this land was guilty of.
Dighton and Forrest, whom I did suborn
To do this ruthless piece of butchery,
Although they were flesh'd[2] villains, bloody dogs,
Melting with tenderness and kind compassion
Wept like two children in their deaths' sad stories.
"Lo, thus," quoth Dighton, "lay those tender babes:"
"Thus, thus," quoth Forrest, "girdling one another
Within their innocent alabaster arms:
Their lips were four red roses on a stalk,
Which in their summer beauty kiss'd each other.
A book of prayers on their pillow lay;
Which once," quoth Forrest, "almost changed my mind;
But O! the devil" — there the villain stopp'd;
Whilst Dighton thus told on: "We smothered
The most replenished[3] sweet work of nature
That from the prime creation e'er she framed."
Thus both are gone with conscience and remorse;
They could not speak; and so I left them both,
To bring this tidings to the bloody king.
And here he comes.

Enter KING RICHARD

                              All hail, my sovereign liege!
K. RICH.   Kind Tyrrel, am I happy in thy news?
TYR.   If to have done the thing you gave in charge
Beget your happiness, be happy then,
For it is done, my lord.
K. RICH.   But didst thou see them dead?
TYR.   I did, my lord.
K. RICH.   And buried, gentle Tyrrel?

---

1. *arch*] consummate, notable.
2. *flesh'd*] inured to bloodshed.
3. *replenished*] complete, perfect.

TYR.   The chaplain of the Tower hath buried them;
        But how or in what place I do not know.
K. RICH.   Come to me, Tyrrel, soon at after supper,[4]
        And thou shalt tell the process of their death.
        Meantime, but think how I may do thee good,
        And be inheritor of thy desire.
        Farewell till soon.   [*Exit* TYRREL.]
        The son of Clarence have I pent up close;
        His daughter meanly have I match'd in marriage;[5]
        The sons of Edward sleep in Abraham's bosom,
        And Anne my wife hath bid the world good night.
        Now, for I know the Breton Richmond aims
        At young Elizabeth, my brother's daughter,
        And, by that knot, looks proudly o'er the crown,
        To her I go, a jolly thriving wooer.

Enter CATESBY

CATE.   My lord!
K. RICH.   Good news or bad, that thou comest in so bluntly?
CATE.   Bad news, my lord: Ely[6] is fled to Richmond;
        And Buckingham, back'd with the hardy Welshmen,
        Is in the field, and still his power increaseth.
K. RICH.   Ely with Richmond troubles me more near
        Than Buckingham and his rash-levied army.
        Come, I have heard that fearful commenting
        Is leaden servitor to dull delay;
        Delay leads impotent and snail-paced beggary:[7]
        Then fiery expedition[8] be my wing,
        Jove's Mercury,[9] and herald for a king!
        Come, muster men: my counsel is my shield;
        We must be brief when traitors brave the field.[10]   [*Exeunt.*]

---

   4. *soon at after supper*] about the time when supper is over.
   5. *His . . . marriage*] Clarence's daughter Margaret was married to Sir Richard Pole, who
      was of somewhat better birth than the text indicates. Contrary to the statement of the
      text, the union took place about 1491, some years after Richard's death, by direction of
      Henry VII.
   6. *Ely*] John Morton, Bishop of Ely, afterwards Archbishop of Canterbury, by the appoint-
      ment of Henry VII.
   7. *fearful . . . beggary*] timorous reflection serves the slow purpose of sluggish procrastina-
      tion; procrastination superinduces feeble and creeping beggary.
   8. *fiery expedition*] rapidity of fire or lightning.
   9. *Mercury*] the swift messenger of Jove.
  10. *brave the field*] vauntingly challenge (us) to the battlefield.

SCENE IV. *Before the Palace.*

Enter QUEEN MARGARET

Q. MAR.　So, now prosperity begins to mellow
　　　　And drop into the rotten mouth of death.
　　　　Here in these confines slily have I lurk'd,
　　　　To watch the waning of mine adversaries.
　　　　A dire induction[1] am I witness to,
　　　　And will to France, hoping the consequence
　　　　Will prove as bitter, black, and tragical.
　　　　Withdraw thee, wretched Margaret: who comes here?

Enter QUEEN ELIZABETH *and the* DUCHESS OF YORK

Q. ELIZ.　Ah, my young princes! ah, my tender babes!
　　　　My unblown flowers, new-appearing sweets!
　　　　If yet your gentle souls fly in the air,
　　　　And be not fix'd in doom perpetual,
　　　　Hover about me with your airy wings,
　　　　And hear your mother's lamentation!
Q. MAR.　Hover about her; say, that right for right
　　　　Hath dimm'd your infant morn to aged night.[2]
DUCH.　So many miseries have crazed my voice,
　　　　That my woe-wearied tongue is mute and dumb.
　　　　Edward Plantagenet, why art thou dead?
Q. MAR.　Plantagenet doth quit[3] Plantagenet,
　　　　Edward for Edward pays a dying debt.
Q. ELIZ.　Wilt thou, O God, fly from such gentle lambs,
　　　　And throw them in the entrails of the wolf?
　　　　When didst thou sleep when such a deed was done?
Q. MAR.　When holy Harry died, and my sweet son.
DUCH.　Blind sight, dead life, poor mortal living ghost,
　　　　Woe's scene, world's shame, grave's due by life usurp'd,
　　　　Brief abstract and record of tedious days,

---

1. *induction*] preparation, prelude.
2. *right for right . . . night*] Supreme right, justice answering the claims of justice, has dimmed or blotted out the bright dawn of your infant's life and put in its place the darkness of death, which commonly awaits old age. The losses which Queen Margaret has suffered cause her to regard Queen Elizabeth's bereavement as just retribution for the removal of her own kindred.
3. *quit*] requite.

Rest thy unrest on England's lawful earth,   [*Sitting down.*]
Unlawfully made drunk with innocents' blood!

Q. ELIZ.   O, that thou wouldst as well afford a grave
As thou canst yield a melancholy seat!
Then would I hide my bones, not rest them here.
O, who hath any cause to mourn but I?   [*Sitting down by her.*]

Q. MAR.   If ancient sorrow[4] be most reverend,
Give mine the benefit of seniory,[5]
And let my woes frown on the upper hand.
If sorrow can admit society,   [*Sitting down with them.*]
Tell o'er your woes again by viewing mine:
I had an Edward, till a Richard kill'd him;
I had a Harry, till a Richard kill'd him:
Thou hadst an Edward, till a Richard kill'd him;
Thou hadst a Richard, till a Richard kill'd him.

DUCH.   I had a Richard too, and thou didst kill him;
I had a Rutland too, thou holp'st to kill him.

Q. MAR.   Thou hadst a Clarence too, and Richard kill'd him.
From forth the kennel of thy womb hath crept
A hell-hound that doth hunt us all to death:
That dog, that had his teeth[6] before his eyes,
To worry lambs and lap their gentle blood,
That foul defacer of God's handiwork,
That excellent grand tyrant of the earth,
That reigns in galled eyes of weeping souls,
Thy womb let loose, to chase us to our graves.
O upright, just, and true-disposing God,
How do I thank thee, that this carnal[7] cur
Preys on the issue of his mother's body,
And makes her pew-fellow[8] with others' moan!

DUCH.   O Harry's wife, triumph not in my woes!
God witness with me, I have wept for thine.

Q. MAR.   Bear with me; I am hungry for revenge,
And now I cloy me with beholding it.
Thy Edward he is dead, that stabb'd my Edward;
Thy other Edward dead, to quit my Edward;
Young York he is but boot,[9] because both they

---

4. *ancient sorrow*] sorrow of age.
5. *seniory*] seniority.
6. *dog . . . teeth*] Richard was reported to have been born with teeth.
7. *carnal*] flesh-consuming, cannibal.
8. *pew-fellow*] companion, comrade, partner.
9. *boot*] a mere trifle (an extra bit of merchandise thrown in by a vendor to entice potential buyers).

Match not the high perfection of my loss:
Thy Clarence he is dead that kill'd my Edward;
And the beholders of this tragic play,
The adulterate[10] Hastings, Rivers, Vaughan, Grey,
Untimely smother'd in their dusky graves.
Richard yet lives, hell's black intelligencer,[11]
Only reserved their[12] factor,[13] to buy souls
And send them thither: but at hand, at hand,
Ensues his piteous and unpitied end:
Earth gapes, hell burns, fiends roar, saints pray,
To have him suddenly convey'd away.
Cancel his bond of life, dear God, I pray,
That I may live to say, The dog is dead!

Q. ELIZ.   O, thou didst prophesy the time would come
That I should wish for thee to help me curse
That bottled spider, that foul bunch-back'd toad!

Q. MAR.   I call'd thee then vain flourish of my fortune;
I call'd thee then poor shadow, painted queen;
The presentation of but what I was;
The flattering index[14] of a direful pageant;
One heaved a-high, to be hurl'd down below;
A mother only mock'd with two sweet babes;
A dream of what thou wert, a breath, a bubble,
A sign of dignity, a garish flag
To be the aim of every dangerous shot;
A queen in jest, only to fill the scene.
Where is thy husband now? where be thy brothers?
Where are thy children? wherein dost thou joy?
Who sues to thee, and cries "God save the queen"?
Where be the bending peers that flattered thee?
Where be the thronging troops that followed thee?
Decline all this,[15] and see what now thou art:
For happy wife, a most distressed widow;
For joyful mother, one that wails the name;
For queen, a very caitiff[16] crown'd with care;
For one being sued to, one that humbly sues;
For one that scorn'd at me, now scorn'd of me;

---

10. *adulterate*] adulterous.
11. *intelligencer*] agent, emissary, informer.
12. *their*] i.e., hell's (treated as a plural because it signifies a community of evil spirits).
13. *factor*] agent (of hell).
14. *index*] prelude.
15. *Decline all this*] Go through all this (as through the declension of a verb or noun in a grammar book).
16. *caitiff*] wretch, slave.

For one being fear'd of all, now fearing one;
For one commanding all, obey'd of none.
Thus hath the course of justice wheel'd about,
And left thee but a very prey to time;
Having no more but thought of what thou wert,
To torture thee the more, being what thou art.
Thou didst usurp my place, and dost thou not
Usurp the just proportion of my sorrow?
Now thy proud neck bears half my burthen'd yoke;
From which even here I slip my weary neck,
And leave the burthen of it all on thee.
Farewell, York's wife, and queen of sad mischance:
These English woes will make me smile in France.

Q. ELIZ.   O thou well skill'd in curses, stay awhile,
And teach me how to curse mine enemies!

Q. MAR.   Forbear to sleep the nights, and fast the days;
Compare dead happiness with living woe;
Think that thy babes were fairer than they were,
And he that slew them fouler than he is:
Bettering thy loss[17] makes the bad causer worse:
Revolving this will teach thee how to curse.

Q. ELIZ.   My words are dull; O, quicken them with thine!

Q. MAR.   Thy woes will make them sharp and pierce like mine. [*Exit.*]

DUCH.   Why should calamity be full of words?

Q. ELIZ.   Windy attorneys to their client woes,
Airy succeeders of intestate joys,[18]
Poor breathing orators of miseries!
Let them have scope: though what they do impart
Help not at all, yet do they ease the heart.

DUCH.   If so, then be not tongue-tied: go with me,
And in the breath of bitter words let's smother
My damned son, which thy two sweet sons smother'd.
I hear his drum: be copious in exclaims.

Enter KING RICHARD, *marching, with drums and trumpets*

K. RICH.   Who intercepts my expedition?

DUCH.   O, she that might have intercepted thee,
By strangling thee in her accursed womb,
From all the slaughters, wretch, that thou hast done!

Q. ELIZ.   Hidest thou that forehead with a golden crown,

---

17. *Bettering thy loss*] exaggeration of thy loss.
18. *Airy succeeders of intestate joys*] breath-born heirs or inheritors of poor joys, which
(with nothing to bequeath) have made no will.

Where should be graven, if that right were right,
The slaughter of the prince that owed[19] that crown,
And the dire death of my two sons and brothers?
Tell me, thou villain slave, where are my children?

DUCH. Thou toad, thou toad, where is thy brother Clarence?
And little Ned Plantagenet, his son?

Q. ELIZ. Where is kind Hastings, Rivers, Vaughan, Grey?

K. RICH. A flourish, trumpets! strike alarum, drums!
Let not the heavens hear these tell-tale women
Rail on the Lord's anointed: strike, I say! [*Flourish. Alarums.*]
Either be patient, and entreat[20] me fair,
Or with the clamorous report of war
Thus will I drown your exclamations.

DUCH. Art thou my son?

K. RICH. Ay, I thank God, my father, and yourself.

DUCH. Then patiently hear my impatience.

K. RICH. Madam, I have a touch of your condition,[21]
Which cannot brook the accent of reproof.

DUCH. O, let me speak!

K. RICH.   Do then; but I'll not hear.

DUCH. I will be mild and gentle in my speech.

K. RICH. And brief, good mother; for I am in haste.

DUCH. Art thou so hasty? I have stay'd for thee,
God knows, in anguish, pain and agony.

K. RICH. And came I not at last to comfort you?

DUCH. No, by the holy rood, thou know'st it well,
Thou camest on earth to make the earth my hell.
A grievous burthen was thy birth to me;
Tetchy[22] and wayward was thy infancy;
Thy school-days frightful,[23] desperate, wild, and furious,
Thy prime of manhood daring, bold, and venturous,
Thy age confirm'd,[24] proud, subtle, bloody, treacherous;
More mild, but yet more harmful, kind in hatred:
What comfortable hour canst thou name,
That ever graced me in thy company?

K. RICH. Faith, none, but Humphrey Hour, that call'd your grace

---

19. *owed*] owned.
20. *entreat*] treat, use.
21. *a touch of your condition*] a dash of your temperament.
22. *Tetchy*] fretful, peevish.
23. *frightful*] causing fright.
24. *Thy age confirm'd*] thy ripened age.

    To breakfast once forth of[25] my company.[26]
    If I be so disgracious in your sight,
    Let me march on, and not offend your grace.
    Strike up the drum.
DUCH.   I prithee, hear me speak.
K. RICH.   You speak too bitterly.
DUCH.   Hear me a word;
    For I shall never speak to thee again.
K. RICH.   So.
DUCH.   Either thou wilt die, by God's just ordinance,
    Ere from this war thou turn a conqueror,
    Or I with grief and extreme age shall perish
    And never look upon thy face again.
    Therefore take with thee my most heavy curse;
    Which, in the day of battle, tire thee more
    Than all the complete armour that thou wear'st!
    My prayers on the adverse party fight;
    And there the little souls of Edward's children
    Whisper the spirits of thine enemies,
    And promise them success and victory.
    Bloody thou art, bloody will be thy end;
    Shame serves thy life and doth thy death attend.   [*Exit.*]
Q. ELIZ.   Though far more cause, yet much less spirit to curse
    Abides in me; I say amen to all.
K. RICH.   Stay, madam; I must speak a word with you.
Q. ELIZ.   I have no moe sons of the royal blood
    For thee to murder: for my daughters, Richard,
    They shall be praying nuns, not weeping queens;
    And therefore level not to hit their lives.
K. RICH.   You have a daughter call'd Elizabeth,
    Virtuous and fair, royal and gracious.
Q. ELIZ.   And must she die for this? O, let her live,
    And I'll corrupt her manners, stain her beauty;
    Slander myself as false to Edward's bed;
    Throw over her the veil of infamy:
    So she may live unscarr'd of bleeding slaughter,
    I will confess she was not Edward's daughter.

---

25. *forth of*] away from.
26. *Humphrey Hour . . . company*] The reference is probably to the hour when the
    Duchess gave birth to Richard, and to the first meal which she took after her delivery.
    According to homely wit, after delivery the mother traditionally breakfasted apart from
    the child whom she had hitherto fed in her womb along with herself. "To dine with the
    Duke of Humphrey," meant to go hungry, to go without one's dinner.

K. RICH.   Wrong not her birth, she is of royal blood.
Q. ELIZ.   To save her life, I'll say she is not so.
K. RICH.   Her life is only safest in her birth.
Q. ELIZ.   And only in that safety died her brothers.
K. RICH.   Lo, at their births good stars were opposite.[27]
Q. ELIZ.   No, to their lives bad friends were contrary.
K. RICH.   All unavoided[28] is the doom of destiny.
Q. ELIZ.   True, when avoided grace makes destiny:
    My babes were destined to a fairer death,
    If grace had bless'd thee with a fairer life.
K. RICH.   You speak as if that I had slain my cousins.
Q. ELIZ.   Cousins, indeed; and by their uncle cozen'd
    Of comfort, kingdom, kindred, freedom, life.
    Whose hand soever lanced their tender hearts,
    Thy head, all indirectly,[29] gave direction:
    No doubt the murderous knife was dull and blunt,
    Till it was whetted on thy stone-hard heart,
    To revel in the entrails of my lambs.
    But that still use[30] of grief makes wild grief tame,
    My tongue should to thy ears not name my boys,
    Till that my nails were anchor'd in thine eyes;
    And I, in such a desperate bay of death,
    Like a poor bark, of sails and tackling reft,
    Rush all to pieces on thy rocky bosom.
K. RICH.   Madam, so thrive I in my enterprise,
    And dangerous success of bloody wars,
    As I intend more good to you and yours,
    Than ever you or yours were by me wrong'd!
Q. ELIZ.   What good is cover'd with the face of heaven,
    To be discover'd, that can do me good?
K. RICH.   The advancement of your children, gentle lady.
Q. ELIZ.   Up to some scaffold, there to lose their heads?
K. RICH.   No, to the dignity and height of honour,
    The high imperial type[31] of this earth's glory.
Q. ELIZ.   Flatter my sorrows with report of it;
    Tell me what state, what dignity, what honour,
    Canst thou demise to any child of mine?
K. RICH.   Even all I have; yea, and myself and all,

---

27. *opposite*] hostile, in opposition; an astrological term.
28. *unavoided*] unavoidable.
29. *indirectly*] wickedly, disingenuously.
30. *still use*] continual habit.
31. *type*] symbol, emblem, crown.

Will I withal endow a child of thine;
So in the Lethe[32] of thy angry soul
Thou drown the sad remembrance of those wrongs,
Which thou supposest I have done to thee.

Q. ELIZ.   Be brief, lest that the process of thy kindness
Last longer telling than thy kindness' date.

K. RICH.   Then know, that from my soul I love thy daughter.

Q. ELIZ.   My daughter's mother thinks it with her soul.

K. RICH.   What do you think?

Q. ELIZ.   That thou dost love my daughter from[33] thy soul:
So from thy soul's love didst thou love her brothers;
And from my heart's love I do thank thee for it.

K. RICH.   Be not so hasty to confound my meaning:
I mean, that with my soul I love thy daughter,
And mean to make her queen of England.

Q. ELIZ.   Say then, who dost thou mean shall be her king?

K. RICH.   Even he that makes her queen: who should be else?

Q. ELIZ.   What, thou?

K. RICH.   I, even I: what think you of it, madam?

Q. ELIZ.   How canst thou woo her?

K. RICH.   That would I learn of you,
As one that are best acquainted with her humour.

Q. ELIZ.   And wilt thou learn of me?

K. RICH.   Madam, with all my heart.

Q. ELIZ.   Send to her, by the man that slew her brothers,
A pair of bleeding hearts; thereon engrave
Edward and York; then haply she will weep:
Therefore present to her, — as sometime Margaret
Did to thy father, steep'd in Rutland's blood, —
A handkerchief; which, say to her, did drain
The purple sap from her sweet brother's body,
And bid her dry her weeping eyes therewith.
If this inducement force her not to love,
Send her a story of thy noble acts;
Tell her thou madest away her uncle Clarence,
Her uncle Rivers; yea, and, for her sake,
Madest quick conveyance with her good aunt Anne.

K. RICH.   Come, come, you mock me; this is not the way
To win your daughter.

Q. ELIZ.   There is no other way;

---

32. *Lethe*] in classical mythology, the river of forgetfulness.
33. *from*] here meaning "away from," as opposed to "from the depths of," which is Richard's use of the preposition.

Unless thou couldst put on some other shape,
And not be Richard that hath done all this.
K. RICH.   Say that I did all this for love of her.
Q. ELIZ.   Nay, then indeed she cannot choose but hate thee,
Having bought love with such a bloody spoil.
K. RICH.   Look, what is done cannot be now amended:
Men shall deal unadvisedly sometimes,
Which after-hours give leisure to repent.
If I did take the kingdom from your sons,
To make amends, I'll give it to your daughter.
If I have kill'd the issue of your womb,
To quicken your increase, I will beget
Mine issue of your blood upon your daughter:
A grandam's name is little less in love
Than is the doting title of a mother;
They are as children but one step below,
Even of your mettle, of your very blood;
Of all one pain, save for a night of groans
Endured of her, for whom you bid like sorrow.[34]
Your children were vexation to your youth,
But mine shall be a comfort to your age.
The loss you have is but a son being king,
And by that loss your daughter is made queen.
I cannot make you what amends I would,
Therefore accept such kindness as I can.
Dorset your son, that with a fearful soul
Leads discontented steps in foreign soil,
This fair alliance quickly shall call home
To high promotions and great dignity:
The king, that calls your beauteous daughter wife,
Familiarly shall call thy Dorset brother;
Again shall you be mother to a king,
And all the ruins of distressful times
Repair'd with double riches of content.
What! we have many goodly days to see:
The liquid drops of tears that you have shed
Shall come again, transform'd to orient pearl,
Advantaging[35] their loan with interest
Of ten times double gain of happiness.
Go then, my mother, to thy daughter go;
Make bold her bashful years with your experience;
Prepare her ears to hear a wooer's tale;

---

34. *Endured . . . sorrow*] endured by her for whom you suffered like grief.
35. *Advantaging*] increasing.

      Put in her tender heart the aspiring flame
      Of golden sovereignty; acquaint the princess
      With the sweet silent hours of marriage joys:
      And when this arm of mine hath chastised
      The petty rebel, dull-brain'd Buckingham,
      Bound with triumphant garlands will I come,
      And lead thy daughter to a conqueror's bed;
      To whom I will retail my conquest won,
      And she shall be sole victress, Cæsar's Cæsar.
Q. ELIZ.   What were I best to say? her father's brother
      Would be her lord? or shall I say, her uncle?
      Or, he that slew her brothers and her uncles?
      Under what title shall I woo for thee,
      That God, the law, my honour and her love,
      Can make seem pleasing to her tender years?
K. RICH.   Infer fair England's peace by this alliance.
Q. ELIZ.   Which she shall purchase with still lasting war.
K. RICH.   Say that the king, which may command, entreats.
Q. ELIZ.   That at her hands which the king's King forbids.
K. RICH.   Say, she shall be a high and mighty queen.
Q. ELIZ.   To wail the title, as her mother doth.
K. RICH.   Say, I will love her everlastingly.
Q. ELIZ.   But how long shall that title "ever" last?
K. RICH.   Sweetly in force unto her fair life's end.
Q. ELIZ.   But how long fairly shall her sweet life last?
K. RICH.   So long as heaven and nature lengthens it.
Q. ELIZ.   So long as hell and Richard likes of it.
K. RICH.   Say, I, her sovereign, am her subject love.
Q. ELIZ.   But she, your subject, loathes such sovereignty.
K. RICH.   Be eloquent in my behalf to her.
Q. ELIZ.   An honest tale speeds best being plainly told.
K. RICH.   Then in plain terms tell her my loving tale.
Q. ELIZ.   Plain and not honest is too harsh a style.
K. RICH.   Your reasons are too shallow and too quick.
Q. ELIZ.   O no, my reasons are too deep and dead;[36]
      Too deep and dead, poor infants, in their grave.
K. RICH.   Harp not on that string, madam; that is past.
Q. ELIZ.   Harp on it still shall I till heart-strings break.
K. RICH.   Now, by my George,[37] my garter, and my crown, —
Q. ELIZ.   Profaned, dishonour'd, and the third usurp'd.

---

36. *quick ... dead*] Richard uses "quick" in its ordinary sense of "rapid," "nimble." Queen
    Elizabeth quibblingly takes it in the sense of "alive," of which "dead" is the negative.
37. *George*] a jewel in the shape of a figure of England's patron saint, which formed part of
    the insignia of the Order of the Garter.

K. Rich. I swear —
Q. Eliz. By nothing; for this is no oath:
  The George, profaned, hath lost his holy honour;
  The garter, blemish'd, pawn'd his knightly virtue;
  The crown, usurp'd, disgraced his kingly glory.
  If something thou wilt swear to be believed,
  Swear then by something that thou hast not wrong'd.
K. Rich. Now, by the world —
Q. Eliz. 'Tis full of thy foul wrongs.
K. Rich. My father's death —
Q. Eliz. Thy life hath that dishonour'd.
K. Rich. Then, by myself —
Q. Eliz. Thyself thyself misusest.
K. Rich. Why then, by God —
Q. Eliz. God's wrong is most of all.
  If thou hadst fear'd to break an oath by Him,
  The unity the king thy brother made
  Had not been broken, nor my brother slain:
  If thou hadst fear'd to break an oath by Him,
  The imperial metal, circling now thy brow,
  Had graced the tender temples of my child,
  And both the princes had been breathing here,
  Which now, two tender playfellows for dust,
  Thy broken faith hath made a prey for worms.
  What canst thou swear by now?
K. Rich. The time to come.
Q. Eliz. That thou hast wronged in the time o'erpast;
  For I myself have many tears to wash
  Hereafter time, for time past wrong'd by thee.
  The children live, whose parents thou hast slaughter'd,
  Ungovern'd youth, to wail it in their age;
  The parents live, whose children thou hast butcher'd,
  Old withered plants, to wail it with their age.
  Swear not by time to come; for that thou hast
  Misused ere used, by time misused o'erpast.[38]
K. Rich. As I intend to prosper and repent,
  So thrive I in my dangerous attempt
  Of hostile arms! myself myself confound!
  Heaven and fortune bar me happy hours!
  Day, yield me not thy light; nor, night, thy rest!
  Be opposite all planets of good luck
  To my proceedings, if, with pure heart's love,

---

38. *for that . . . o'erpast*] for thou hast misused the future before it was at your disposal, by
  virtue of the misuse to which you have put the time that is over and past.

        Immaculate devotion, holy thoughts,
        I tender not thy beauteous princely daughter!
        In her consists my happiness and thine;
        Without her, follows to this land and me,
        To thee, herself, and many a Christian soul,
        Death, desolation, ruin and decay:
        It cannot be avoided but by this;
        It will not be avoided but by this.
        Therefore, good mother, — I must call you so —
        Be the attorney of my love to her:
        Plead what I will be, not what I have been;
        Not my deserts, but what I will deserve:
        Urge the necessity and state of times,
        And be not peevish-fond[39] in great designs.
Q. ELIZ.   Shall I be tempted of the devil thus?
K. RICH.   Ay, if the devil tempt thee to do good.
Q. ELIZ.   Shall I forget myself to be myself?
K. RICH.   Ay, if yourself's remembrance wrong yourself.
Q. ELIZ.   But thou didst kill my children.
K. RICH.   But in your daughter's womb I bury them:
        Where in that nest of spicery[40] they shall breed
        Selves of themselves, to your recomforture.[41]
Q. ELIZ.   Shall I go win my daughter to thy will?
K. RICH.   And be a happy mother by the deed.
Q. ELIZ.   I go. Write to me very shortly,
        And you shall understand from me her mind.
K. RICH.   Bear her my true love's kiss; and so, farewell.
                           [Exit QUEEN ELIZABETH.]
        Relenting fool, and shallow, changing woman!

Enter RATCLIFF; CATESBY *following*

        How now! what news?
RAT.   My gracious sovereign, on the western coast
        Rideth a puissant[42] navy; to the shore
        Throng many doubtful hollow-hearted friends,
        Unarm'd, and unresolved to beat them back:
        'Tis thought that Richmond is their admiral;

---

39. *peevish-fond*] perversely stupid.
40. *nest of spicery*] an allusion to the fable of the phœnix, which was consumed every thousand years on a funeral pyre of spices on which the bird was at the same time reincarnated.
41. *recomforture*] comfort, consolation.
42. *puissant*] mighty, powerful.

And there they hull,[43] expecting but the aid
Of Buckingham to welcome them ashore.
K. RICH.   Some light-foot friend post to the Duke of Norfolk:
Ratcliff, thyself, or Catesby; where is he?
CATE.   Here, my lord.
K. RICH.   Fly to the duke. [*To* RATCLIFF] Post thou to Salisbury:
When thou comest thither, — [*To* CATESBY] Dull unmindful villain,
Why stand'st thou still, and go'st not to the duke?
CATE.   First, mighty sovereign, let me know your mind,
What from your grace I shall deliver to him.
K. RICH.   O, true, good Catesby: bid him levy[44] straight
The greatest strength and power he can make,
And meet me presently[45] at Salisbury.
CATE.   I go.   [*Exit.*]
RAT.   What is't your highness' pleasure I shall do
At Salisbury?
K. RICH.   Why, what wouldst thou do there before I go?
RAT.   Your highness told me I should post before.
K. RICH.   My mind is changed, sir, my mind is changed.

Enter LORD STANLEY

How now, what news with you?
STAN.   None good, my lord, to please you with the hearing;
Nor none so bad, but it may well be told.
K. RICH.   Hoyday,[46] a riddle! neither good nor bad!
Why dost thou run so many mile about,
When thou mayst tell thy tale a nearer way?
Once more, what news?
STAN.   Richmond is on the seas.
K. RICH.   There let him sink, and be the seas on him!
White-liver'd runagate,[47] what doth he there?
STAN.   I know not, mighty sovereign, but by guess.
K. RICH.   Well, sir, as you guess, as you guess?
STAN.   Stirr'd up by Dorset, Buckingham, and Ely,
He makes for England, there to claim the crown.
K. RICH.   Is the chair empty? is the sword unsway'd?
Is the king dead? the empire unpossess'd?
What heir of York is there alive but we?
And who is England's king but great York's heir?

---

43. *hull*] to float, drift with sails furled.
44. *levy*] raise (an army).
45. *presently*] immediately.
46. *Hoyday*] an exclamation of contemptuous surprise.
47. *White-liver'd runagate*] cowardly runaway.

Then, tell me, what doth he upon the sea?

STAN.   Unless for that, my liege, I cannot guess.

K. RICH.   Unless for that he comes to be your liege,
You cannot guess wherefore the Welshman[48] comes.
Thou wilt revolt and fly to him, I fear.

STAN.   No, mighty liege; therefore mistrust me not.

K. RICH.   Where is thy power then to beat him back?
Where are thy tenants and thy followers?
Are they not now upon the western shore,
Safe-conducting the rebels from their ships?

STAN.   No, my good lord, my friends are in the north.

K. RICH.   Cold friends to Richard: what do they in the north,
When they should serve their sovereign in the west?

STAN.   They have not been commanded, mighty sovereign:
Please it your majesty to give me leave,
I'll muster up my friends, and meet your grace
Where and what time your majesty shall please.

K. RICH.   Ay, ay, thou wouldst be gone to join with Richmond:
I will not trust you, sir.

STAN.   Most mighty sovereign,
You have no cause to hold my friendship doubtful:
I never was nor never will be false.

K. RICH.   Well,
Go muster men; but, hear you, leave behind
Your son, George Stanley: look your faith be firm,
Or else his head's assurance is but frail.

STAN.   So deal with him as I prove true to you.   [*Exit.*]

Enter a Messenger

MESS.   My gracious sovereign, now in Devonshire,
As I by friends am well advertised,[49]
Sir Edward Courtney, and the haughty prelate
Bishop of Exeter, his brother there,[50]
With many moe confederates, are in arms.

Enter another Messenger

SEC. MESS.   My liege, in Kent, the Guildfords are in arms;

---

48. *the Welshman*] i.e., Richmond. Richmond's grandfather was Owen Tudor, who married the widow of Henry V, Catharine of France. Richmond was descended on the maternal side through the Beauforts to John of Gaunt (son of Edward III) and Catherine Swynford, from which connection he derived his claim to the throne.

49. *advertised*] informed, notified. The accents fall on the second and fourth syllables.

50. *brother there*] Peter Courtney, the Bishop of Exeter, was cousin, *not* brother, of Sir Edward Courtney.

And every hour more competitors[51]
Flock to their aid, and still their power increaseth.

Enter another Messenger

THIRD MESS.   My lord, the army of the Duke of Buckingham —
K. RICH.   Out on you, owls! nothing but songs of death?

[*He striketh him.*]

Take that, until thou bring me better news.
THIRD MESS.   The news I have to tell your majesty
Is, that by sudden floods and fall of waters,
Buckingham's army is dispersed and scatter'd;
And he himself wander'd away alone,
No man knows whither.
K. RICH.   I cry thee mercy:
There is my purse to cure that blow of thine.
Hath any well-advised friend proclaim'd
Reward to him that brings the traitor in?
THIRD MESS.   Such proclamation hath been made, my liege.

Enter another Messenger

FOURTH MESS.   Sir Thomas Lovel and Lord Marquess Dorset,
'Tis said, my liege, in Yorkshire are in arms.
Yet this good comfort bring I to your grace,
The Breton navy is dispersed by tempest:
Richmond, in Dorsetshire, sent out a boat
Unto the shore, to ask those on the banks
If they were his assistants, yea or no;
Who answer'd him, they came from Buckingham
Upon his party:[52] he, mistrusting them,
Hoised sail and made away for Brittany.
K. RICH.   March on, march on, since we are up in arms;
If not to fight with foreign enemies,
Yet to beat down these rebels here at home.

Re-enter CATESBY

CATE.   My liege, the Duke of Buckingham is taken;
That is the best news: that the Earl of Richmond
Is with a mighty power landed at Milford,
Is colder tidings, yet they must be told.
K. RICH.   Away towards Salisbury! while we reason here,

---

51. *competitors*] confederates, associates.
52. *Upon his party*] to join his party, to take his side.

A royal battle might be won and lost:
Some one take order[53] Buckingham be brought
To Salisbury; the rest march on with me.   [*Flourish. Exeunt.*]

SCENE V. *Lord Derby's House.*

Enter DERBY *and* SIR CHRISTOPHER URSWICK[1]

DER.   Sir Christopher, tell Richmond this from me:
        That in the sty of this most bloody boar
        My son George Stanley is frank'd up[2] in hold:
        If I revolt, off goes young George's head;
        The fear of that withholds my present aid.
        But, tell me, where is princely Richmond now?
CHRIS.   At Pembroke, or at Ha'rford-west,[3] in Wales.
DER.   What men of name resort to him?
CHRIS.   Sir Walter Herbert, a renowned soldier;
        Sir Gilbert Talbot, Sir William Stanley;
        Oxford, redoubted Pembroke, Sir James Blunt,
        And Rice ap Thomas, with a valiant crew,
        And many moe of noble fame and worth:
        And towards London they do bend their course,
        If by the way they be not fought withal.
DER.   Return unto thy lord; commend me to him:
        Tell him the queen hath heartily consented
        He shall espouse Elizabeth her daughter.
        These letters will resolve[4] him of my mind.
        Farewell.   [*Exeunt.*]

---

53. *take order*] take measures, arrange.

---

1. *Sir Christopher Urswick*] a priest in the service of the Countess of Richmond, and
   employed by her in confidential communication with her son.
2. *frank'd up*] cooped up, confined.
3. *Ha'rford-west*] Haverfordwest, on the coast of Pembrokeshire.
4. *resolve*] inform, satisfy.

ACT V.

SCENE I. *Salisbury. An open place.*

Enter the Sheriff, *and* BUCKINGHAM, *with halberds, led to execution*

BUCK.   Will not King Richard let me speak with him?
SHER.   No, my good lord; therefore be patient.
BUCK.   Hastings, and Edward's children, Rivers, Grey,
    Holy King Henry, and thy fair son Edward,
    Vaughan, and all that have miscarried
    By underhand corrupted foul injustice,
    If that your moody discontented souls
    Do through the clouds behold this present hour,
    Even for revenge mock my destruction!
    This is All-Souls' day,[1] fellows, is it not?
SHER.   It is, my lord.
BUCK.   Why, then All-Souls' day is my body's doomsday.
    This is the day that, in King Edward's time,
    I wish'd might fall on me when I was found
    False to his children or his wife's allies;
    This is the day wherein I wish'd to fall
    By the false faith of him I trusted most;
    This, this All-Souls' day to my fearful soul
    Is the determined respite of my wrongs:[2]
    That high All-seer that I dallied with
    Hath turn'd my feigned prayer on my head,
    And given in earnest what I begg'd in jest.
    Thus doth he force the swords of wicked men
    To turn their own points on their masters' bosoms:
    Now Margaret's curse is fallen upon my head;
    "When he," quoth she, "shall split thy heart with sorrow,
    Remember Margaret was a prophetess."
    Come, sirs, convey me to the block of shame;
    Wrong hath but wrong, and blame the due of blame. [*Exeunt.*]

---

1. *All-Souls' day*] November 2 was the festival day appointed by the Roman Catholic Church in honor of the souls of all the dead, and was believed to be a time when spirits communicated with the living.
2. *determined . . . wrongs*] the term or close of the period to which the punishment of my offences was postponed.

SCENE II. *The Camp near Tamworth.*

Enter RICHMOND, OXFORD, BLUNT, HERBERT, *and others, with drum and colours*

RICHM.   Fellows in arms, and my most loving friends,
    Bruised underneath the yoke of tyranny,
    Thus far into the bowels of the land
    Have we march'd on without impediment;
    And here receive we from our father Stanley
    Lines of fair comfort and encouragement.
    The wretched, bloody, and usurping boar,
    That spoil'd your summer fields and fruitful vines,
    Swills your warm blood like wash,[1] and makes his trough
    In your embowell'd[2] bosoms, this foul swine
    Lies[3] now even in the centre of this isle,
    Near to the town of Leicester, as we learn:
    From Tamworth thither is but one day's march.
    In God's name, cheerly on, courageous friends,
    To reap the harvest of perpetual peace
    By this one bloody trial of sharp war.
OXF.   Every man's conscience is a thousand swords,
    To fight against that bloody homicide.
HERB.   I doubt not but his friends will fly to us.
BLUNT.   He hath no friends but who are friends for fear,
    Which in his greatest need will shrink from him.
RICHM.   All for our vantage. Then, in God's name, march:
    True hope is swift, and flies with swallow's wings;
    Kings it makes gods, and meaner creatures kings.   [*Exeunt.*]

---

1. *Swills . . . like wash*] drinks . . . as a boar sucks up hogwash.
2. *embowell'd*] ripped up, disembowelled.
3. *Lies*] sojourns.

SCENE III. *Bosworth Field.*

Enter KING RICHARD *in arms with* NORFOLK, *the* EARL OF SURREY, *and others*

K. RICH.   Here pitch our tents, even here in Bosworth field.
      My Lord of Surrey, why look you so sad?
SUR.   My heart is ten times lighter than my looks.
K. RICH.   My Lord of Norfolk, —
NOR.   Here, most gracious liege.
K. RICH.   Norfolk, we must have knocks; ha! must we not?
NOR.   We must both give and take, my gracious lord.
K. RICH.   Up with my tent there! here will I lie to-night:
      But where to-morrow? Well, all's one for that.
      Who hath descried the number of the foe?
NOR.   Six or seven thousand is their utmost power.
K. RICH.   Why, our battalion trebles that account:
      Besides, the king's name is a tower of strength,
      Which they upon the adverse party want.[1]
      Up with my tent there! Valiant gentlemen,
      Let us survey the vantage of the field;
      Call for some men of sound direction:[2]
      Let's want no discipline, make no delay;
      For, lords, to-morrow is a busy day.   [*Exeunt.*]

Enter, on the other side of the field, RICHMOND, SIR WILLIAM BRANDON, OXFORD, *and others. Some of the* Soldiers *pitch Richmond's tent*

RICHM.   The weary sun hath made a golden set,
      And by the bright track of his fiery car
      Gives signal of a goodly day to-morrow.
      Sir William Brandon, you shall bear my standard.
      Give me some ink and paper in my tent:
      I'll draw the form and model of our battle,
      Limit each leader to his several charge,
      And part in just proportion our small strength.
      My Lord of Oxford, you, Sir William Brandon,
      And you, Sir Walter Herbert, stay with me.
      The Earl of Pembroke keeps[3] his regiment:

---

1. *want*] lack.
2. *sound direction*] sound judgment, tried skill in leadership.
3. *keeps*] stays with.

    Good Captain Blunt, bear my good-night to him,
    And by the second hour in the morning
    Desire the earl to see me in my tent:
    Yet one thing more, good Blunt, before thou go'st,
    Where is Lord Stanley quarter'd, dost thou know?
BLUNT.   Unless I have mista'en his colours much,
    Which well I am assured I have not done,
    His regiment lies half a mile at least
    South from the mighty power of the king.
RICHM.   If without peril it be possible,
    Good Captain Blunt, bear my good-night to him,
    And give him from me this most needful scroll.
BLUNT.   Upon my life, my lord, I'll undertake it;
    And so, God give you quiet rest to-night!
RICHM.   Good night, good Captain Blunt. Come, gentlemen,
    Let us consult upon to-morrow's business:
    In to our tent! the air is raw and cold.

                       [They withdraw into the tent.]

Enter, to his tent, KING RICHARD, NORFOLK, RATCLIFF, CATESBY, *and others*

K. RICH.   What is't o'clock?
CATE.   It's supper-time, my lord;
    It's nine o'clock.
K. RICH.   I will not sup to-night.
    Give me some ink and paper.
    What, is my beaver[4] easier[5] than it was!
    And all my armour laid into my tent?
CATE.   It is, my liege; and all things are in readiness.
K. RICH.   Good Norfolk, hie thee to thy charge;
    Use careful watch, choose trusty sentinels.
NOR.   I go, my lord.
K. RICH.   Stir with the lark to-morrow, gentle Norfolk.   *[Exit.]*
NOR.   I warrant you, my lord.
K. RICH.   Catesby!
CATE.   My lord?
K. RICH.   Send out a pursuivant at arms
    To Stanley's regiment; bid him bring his power
    Before sunrising, lest his son George fall
    Into the blind cave of eternal night.   *[Exit* CATESBY.*]*
    Fill me a bowl of wine. Give me a watch.[6]

---

4. *beaver*] properly the part of the helmet that could be drawn up and down over the face, but often used for the helmet itself.
5. *easier*] more loosely fitting.
6. *watch*] watchlight, candle.

Saddle white Surrey[7] for the field to-morrow.
Look that my staves[8] be sound, and not too heavy.
Ratcliff!

RAT.   My lord?

K. RICH.   Saw'st thou the melancholy Lord Northumberland?

RAT.   Thomas the Earl of Surrey, and himself,
Much about cock-shut time,[9] from troop to troop
Went through the army, cheering up the soldiers.

K. RICH.   So, I am satisfied. Give me a bowl of wine:
I have not that alacrity of spirit,
Nor cheer of mind, that I was wont to have.
Set it down. Is ink and paper ready?

RAT.   It is, my lord.

K. RICH.   Bid my guard watch. Leave me. Ratcliff,
About the mid of night come to my tent,
And help to arm me. Leave me, I say.

> [*Exeunt* RATCLIFF *and the other attendants.*]

Enter DERBY *to* RICHMOND *in his tent, Lords and others attending*

DER.   Fortune and victory sit on thy helm!

RICHM.   All comfort that the dark night can afford
Be to thy person, noble father-in-law!
Tell me, how fares our loving mother?

DER.   I, by attorney,[10] bless thee from thy mother,
Who prays continually for Richmond's good:
So much for that. The silent hours steal on,
And flaky darkness[11] breaks within the east.
In brief, for so the season bids us be,
Prepare thy battle early in the morning,
And put thy fortune to the arbitrement[12]
Of bloody strokes and mortal-staring[13] war.
I, as I may—that which I would I cannot,—
With best advantage will deceive the time,
And aid thee in this doubtful shock of arms:
But on thy side I may not be too forward,
Lest, being seen, thy brother, tender George,
Be executed in his father's sight.

---

7. *white Surrey*] According to historical sources, Richard was "mounted on a great white courser." The horse's name was presumably Shakespeare's invention.

8. *staves*] the wooden shafts of the lances.

9. *cock-shut time*] twilight.

10. *by attorney*] by deputy, messenger.

11. *flaky darkness*] darkness streaked with light.

12. *arbitrement*] decision.

13. *mortal-staring*] looking with deadly glance.

Farewell: the leisure[14] and the fearful time
Cuts off the ceremonious vows of love,
And ample interchange of sweet discourse,
Which so long sunder'd friends should dwell upon:
God give us leisure for these rites of love!
Once more, adieu: be valiant, and speed well!
RICHM.   Good lords, conduct him to his regiment:
I'll strive, with troubled thoughts, to take a nap,
Lest leaden slumber peise[15] me down to-morrow,
When I should mount with wings of victory:
Once more, good night, kind lords and gentlemen.
                         [*Exeunt all but* RICHMOND.]
O Thou, whose captain I account myself,
Look on my forces with a gracious eye;
Put in their hands thy bruising irons of wrath,
That they may crush down with a heavy fall
The usurping helmets of our adversaries!
Make us thy ministers of chastisement,
That we may praise thee in the victory!
To thee I do commend my watchful soul,
Ere I let fall the windows of mine eyes:
Sleeping and waking, O, defend me still!   [*Sleeps.*]

Enter the Ghost of PRINCE EDWARD, *son to* HENRY THE SIXTH

GHOST.   [*To* RICHARD] Let me sit heavy on thy soul to-morrow!
Think, how thou stab'dst me in my prime of youth
At Tewksbury: despair, therefore, and die!
[*To* RICHMOND] Be cheerful, Richmond; for the wronged souls
Of butcher'd princes fight in thy behalf:
King Henry's issue, Richmond, comforts thee.

Enter the Ghost of HENRY THE SIXTH

GHOST.   [*To* RICHARD] When I was mortal, my anointed body
By thee was punched full of deadly holes:
Think on the Tower and me: despair, and die!
Harry the Sixth bids thee despair and die!
[*To* RICHMOND] Virtuous and holy, be thou conqueror!
Harry, that prophesied thou shouldst be king,
Doth comfort thee in thy sleep: live, and flourish!

Enter the Ghost of CLARENCE

GHOST.   [*To* RICHARD] Let me sit heavy on thy soul to-morrow!

---

14. *leisure*] time at our free disposal.
15. *peise*] weigh.

I, that was wash'd to death with fulsome wine,[16]
Poor Clarence, by thy guile betray'd to death.
To-morrow in the battle think on me,
And fall thy edgeless sword: despair, and die!
[*To* RICHMOND] Thou offspring of the house of Lancaster,
The wronged heirs of York do pray for thee:
Good angels guard thy battle! live, and flourish!

Enter the Ghosts of RIVERS, GREY, *and* VAUGHAN

GHOST OF R.　[*To* RICHARD] Let me sit heavy on thy soul to-morrow,
　　Rivers, that died at Pomfret! despair, and die!
GHOST OF G.　[*To* RICHARD] Think upon Grey, and let thy soul despair!
GHOST OF V.　[*To* RICHARD] Think upon Vaughan, and, with guilty
　　fear,
　　Let fall thy lance: despair, and die!
ALL.　[*To* RICHMOND] Awake, and think our wrongs in Richard's bosom
　　Will conquer him! awake, and win the day!

Enter the Ghost of HASTINGS

GHOST.　[*To* RICHARD] Bloody and guilty, guiltily awake,
　　And in a bloody battle end thy days!
　　Think on Lord Hastings: despair, and die!
　　[*To* RICHMOND] Quiet untroubled soul, awake, awake!
　　Arm, fight, and conquer, for fair England's sake!

Enter the Ghosts of the two young Princes

GHOSTS.　[*To* RICHARD] Dream on thy cousins smothered in the Tower:
　　Let us be lead within thy bosom, Richard,
　　And weigh thee down to ruin, shame, and death!
　　Thy nephews' souls bid thee despair and die!
　　[*To* RICHMOND] Sleep, Richmond, sleep in peace, and wake in joy;
　　Good angels guard thee from the boar's annoy![17]
　　Live, and beget a happy race of kings!
　　Edward's unhappy sons do bid thee flourish.

Enter the Ghost of LADY ANNE *his wife*

GHOST.　[*To* RICHARD] Richard, thy wife, that wretched Anne thy wife,
　　That never slept a quiet hour with thee,
　　Now fills thy sleep with perturbations:
　　To-morrow in the battle think on me,
　　And fall thy edgeless sword: despair, and die!
　　[*To* RICHMOND] Thou quiet soul, sleep thou a quiet sleep:

16. *fulsome wine*] abundance or surfeit of wine.
17. *boar's annoy*] injury from the boar, i.e. Richard.

Dream of success and happy victory!
Thy adversary's wife doth pray for thee.

Enter the Ghost of BUCKINGHAM

GHOST.   [*To* RICHARD] The first was I that help'd thee to the crown;
The last was I that felt thy tyranny:
O, in the battle think on Buckingham,
And die in terror of thy guiltiness!
Dream on, dream on, of bloody deeds and death:
Fainting, despair; despairing, yield thy breath!
[*To* RICHMOND] I died for hope[18] ere I could lend thee aid:
But cheer thy heart, and be thou not dismay'd:
God and good angels fight on Richmond's side;
And Richard falls in height of all his pride.
        [*The Ghosts vanish.* KING RICHARD *starts out of his dream.*]
K. RICH.   Give me another horse: bind up my wounds.
Have mercy, Jesu! — Soft! I did but dream.
O coward conscience, how dost thou afflict me!
The lights burn blue.[19] It is now dead midnight.
Cold fearful drops stand on my trembling flesh.
What do I fear? myself? there's none else by:
Richard loves Richard; that is, I am I.
Is there a murderer here? No. Yes, I am:
Then fly. What, from myself? Great reason why:
Lest I revenge. What, myself upon myself?
Alack, I love myself. Wherefore? for any good
That I myself have done unto myself?
O, no! alas, I rather hate myself
For hateful deeds committed by myself!
I am a villain: yet I lie, I am not.
Fool, of thyself speak well: fool, do not flatter.
My conscience hath a thousand several tongues,
And every tongue brings in a several tale,
And every tale condemns me for a villain.
Perjury, perjury, in the high'st degree;
Murder, stern murder, in the direst degree;
All several sins, all used in each degree,
Throng to the bar,[20] crying all "Guilty! guilty!"
I shall despair. There is no creature loves me;
And if I die, no soul will pity me:
Nay, wherefore should they, since that I myself

---

18. *for hope*] for lack of hope, in despair.
19. *lights burn blue*] thought to be the usual effect of ghostly apparitions.
20. *bar*] the railing at which prisoners stand when on trial.

Find in myself no pity to myself?
Methought the souls of all that I had murder'd
Came to my tent, and every one did threat
To-morrow's vengeance on the head of Richard.

Enter RATCLIFF

RAT.   My lord!
K. RICH.   'Zounds! who is there?
RAT.   Ratcliff, my lord; 'tis I. The early village-cock
Hath twice done salutation to the morn;
Your friends are up, and buckle on their armour.
K. RICH.   O Ratcliff, I have dream'd a fearful dream!
What thinkest thou, will our friends prove all true?
RAT.   No doubt, my lord.
K. RICH.   O Ratcliff, I fear, I fear, —
RAT.   Nay, good my lord, be not afraid of shadows.
K. RICH.   By the apostle Paul, shadows to-night
Have struck more terror to the soul of Richard,
Than can the substance of ten thousand soldiers
Armed in proof,[21] and led by shallow Richmond.
It is not yet near day. Come, go with me;
Under our tents I'll play the eaves-dropper,
To see if any mean to shrink from me.   [*Exeunt.*]

Enter the Lords *to* RICHMOND, *sitting in his tent*

LORDS.   Good morrow, Richmond!
RICHM.   Cry mercy, lords and watchful gentlemen,
That you have ta'en a tardy sluggard here.
LORDS.   How have you slept, my lord?
RICHM.   The sweetest sleep, and fairest-boding dreams
That ever enter'd in a drowsy head,
Have I since your departure had, my lords.
Methought their souls, whose bodies Richard murder'd,
Came to my tent, and cried on[22] victory:
I promise you, my soul is very jocund
In the remembrance of so fair a dream.
How far into the morning is it, lords?
LORDS.   Upon the stroke of four.
RICHM.   Why, then 'tis time to arm and give direction.

---

21. *Armed in proof*] equipped in proved, tested armour.
22. *cried on*] called out.

His oration to his soldiers

More than I have said, loving countrymen,
The leisure and enforcement of the time
Forbids to dwell upon: yet remember this,
God and our good cause fight upon our side;
The prayers of holy saints and wronged souls,
Like high-rear'd bulwarks, stand before our faces.
Richard except, those whom we fight against
Had rather have us win than him they follow:
For what is he they follow? truly, gentlemen,
A bloody tyrant and a homicide;
One raised in blood, and one in blood establish'd;
One that made means to come by what he hath,
And slaughter'd those that were the means to help him;
A base foul stone, made precious by the foil
Of England's chair, where he is falsely set;[23]
One that hath ever been God's enemy:
Then, if you fight against God's enemy,
God will in justice ward you as his soldiers;
If you do sweat to put a tyrant down,
You sleep in peace, the tyrant being slain;
If you do fight against your country's foes,
Your country's fat[24] shall pay your pains the hire;
If you do fight in safeguard of your wives,
Your wives shall welcome home the conquerors;
If you do free your children from the sword,
Your children's children quit[25] it in your age.
Then, in the name of God and all these rights,
Advance your standards, draw your willing swords.
For me, the ransom of my bold attempt[26]
Shall be this cold corpse on the earth's cold face;
But if I thrive, the gain of my attempt
The least of you shall share his part thereof.
Sound drums and trumpets boldly and cheerfully;
God and Saint George! Richmond and victory!   [*Exeunt.*]

Re-enter KING RICHARD, RATCLIFF, *Attendants and Forces*

K. RICH.   What said Northumberland as touching Richmond?

---

23. *chair . . . set*] throne . . . set, as in a jewel.
24. *fat*] wealth.
25. *quit*] requite.
26. *the ransom . . . attempt*] the fine due from me in requital of my boldness.

RAT.   That he was never trained up in arms.

K. RICH.   He said the truth: and what said Surrey, then?

RAT.   He smiled and said "The better for our purpose."

K. RICH.   He was in the right; and so indeed it is.

[The clock striketh.]

Tell the clock there. Give me a calendar.
Who saw the sun to-day?

RAT.   Not I, my lord.

K. RICH.   Then he disdains to shine; for by the book[27]
He should have braved[28] the east an hour ago:
A black day will it be to somebody.
Ratcliff!

RAT.   My lord?

K. RICH.   The sun will not be seen'to-day;
The sky doth frown and lour upon our army.
I would these dewy tears were from the ground.
Not shine to-day! Why, what is that to me
More than to Richmond? for the selfsame heaven
That frowns on me looks sadly upon him.

Re-enter NORFOLK

NOR.   Arm, arm, my lord; the foe vaunts in the field.

K. RICH.   Come, bustle, bustle. Caparison my horse.
Call up Lord Stanley, bid him bring his power:
I will lead forth my soldiers to the plain,
And thus my battle shall be ordered:
My foreward[29] shall be drawn out all in length,
Consisting equally of horse and foot;
Our archers shall be placed in the midst:
John Duke of Norfolk, Thomas Earl of Surrey,
Shall have the leading of this foot and horse.
They thus directed, we will follow
In the main battle, whose puissance[30] on either side
Shall be well winged with our chiefest horse.
This, and Saint George to boot![31] What think'st thou, Norfolk?

NOR.   A good direction, warlike sovereign.
This found I on my tent this morning.

---

27. *book*] almanac.
28. *braved*] made splendid, glorified.
29. *foreward*] vanguard.
30. *puissance*] armed force.
31. *This, and Saint George to boot!*] this order of battle and the favour of our patron saint in addition!

[*He sheweth him a paper.*]

K. RICH.   [*Reads*] "Jockey of Norfolk, be not so bold,
For Dickon[32] thy master is bought and sold."
A thing devised by the enemy.
Go, gentlemen, every man unto his charge:
Let not our babbling dreams affright our souls:
Conscience is but a word that cowards use,
Devised at first to keep the strong in awe:
Our strong arms be our conscience, swords our law.
March on, join bravely, let us to't pell-mell;
If not to heaven, then hand in hand to hell.

His oration to his Army

What shall I say more than I have inferr'd?[33]
Remember whom you are to cope withal;
A sort[34] of vagabonds, rascals, and runaways,
A scum of Bretons, and base lackey peasants,
Whom their o'er-cloyed country vomits forth
To desperate ventures and assured destruction.
You sleeping safe, they bring to you unrest;
You having lands and blest with beauteous wives,
They would restrain[35] the one, distain the other.
And who doth lead them but a paltry fellow,
Long kept in Bretagne at our mother's cost?[36]
A milk-sop, one that never in his life
Felt so much cold as over shoes in snow?
Let's whip these stragglers o'er the seas again,
Lash hence these overweening rags of France,
These famish'd beggars, weary of their lives,
Who, but for dreaming on this fond exploit,
For want of means, poor rats, had hang'd themselves:
If we be conquer'd, let men conquer us,
And not these bastard Bretons, whom our fathers

---

32. *Dickon*] a colloquial form of Richard. "Bought and sold" means "betrayed."
33. *inferr'd*] alleged.
34. *sort*] set, company.
35. *restrain*] put restraint on, withhold from lawful owners.
36. *our mother's*] Shakespeare is following Richard's speech as it appears in the *second* edition of Holinshed's *Chronicle*, where Richmond is said to have been "brought up by *my moothers* meanes . . . in the court of Francis, Duke of Britaine." Hall's *Chronicle* and the *first* edition of Holinshed read *brother's* for *mother's*. There is little doubt that *brother's* is the right reading. Richard's brother, King Edward IV, had arranged with the Duke of Brittany for Richmond to reside at his court.

Have in their own land beaten, bobb'd,[37] and thump'd,
And in record left them the heirs of shame.
Shall these enjoy our lands? lie with our wives?
Ravish our daughters? [*Drum afar off.*] Hark! I hear their drum.
Fight, gentlemen of England! fight, bold yeomen!
Draw, archers, draw your arrows to the head!
Spur your proud horses hard, and ride in blood;
Amaze the welkin[38] with your broken staves!

Enter a Messenger

What says Lord Stanley? will he bring his power?[39]
MESS.   My lord, he doth deny to come.
K. RICH.   Off with his son George's head!
NOR.   My lord, the enemy is past the marsh:
    After the battle let George Stanley die.
K. RICH.   A thousand hearts are great within my bosom:
    Advance our standards, set upon our foes;
    Our ancient word of courage, fair Saint George,
    Inspire us with the spleen of fiery dragons!
    Upon them! Victory sits on our helms.   [*Exeunt.*]

SCENE IV. *Another Part of the Field.*

Alarum: excursions. Enter NORFOLK *and forces fighting; to him* CATESBY

CATE.   Rescue, my Lord of Norfolk, rescue, rescue!
    The king enacts more wonders than a man,
    Daring an opposite[1] to every danger:
    His horse is slain, and all on foot he fights,
    Seeking for Richmond in the throat of death.
    Rescue, fair lord, or else the day is lost!

Alarums. Enter KING RICHARD

K. RICH.   A horse! a horse! my kingdom for a horse!
CATE.   Withdraw, my lord; I'll help you to a horse.
K. RICH.   Slave, I have set my life upon a cast,

---

37. *bobb'd*] buffeted.
38. *the welkin*] the skies.
39. *power*] force, army.

---

1. *Daring an opposite*] venturing to oppose himself.

And I will stand the hazard of the die.
I think there be six Richmonds in the field;
Five have I slain to-day instead of him.
A horse! a horse! my kingdom for a horse!   [*Exeunt.*]

SCENE V. *Another Part of the Field.*

Alarum. Enter RICHARD *and* RICHMOND; *they fight.* RICHARD *is slain. Retreat and flourish. Re-enter* RICHMOND, DERBY *bearing the crown, with divers other Lords*

RICHM.   God and your arms be praised, victorious friends!
    The day is ours; the bloody dog is dead.
DER.   Courageous Richmond, well hast thou acquit thee.
    Lo, here, this long usurped royalty
    From the dead temples of this bloody wretch
    Have I pluck'd off, to grace thy brows withal:
    Wear it, enjoy it, and make much of it.
RICHM.   Great God of heaven, say amen to all!
    But, tell me, is young George Stanley living?
DER.   He is, my lord, and safe in Leicester town;
    Whither, if it please you, we may now withdraw us.
RICHM.   What men of name are slain on either side?
DER.   John Duke of Norfolk, Walter Lord Ferrers, Sir Robert Braken-
    bury, and Sir William Brandon.
RICH.   Inter their bodies as becomes their births:
    Proclaim a pardon to the soldiers fled,
    That in submission will return to us:
    And then, as we have ta'en the sacrament,
    We will unite the white rose and the red.
    Smile heaven upon this fair conjunction,
    That long have frown'd upon their enmity!
    What traitor hears me, and says not amen?
    England hath long been mad, and scarr'd herself;
    The brother blindly shed the brother's blood,
    The father rashly slaughter'd his own son,
    The son, compell'd, been butcher to the sire:
    All this divided York and Lancaster,
    Divided in their dire division,
    O, now let Richmond and Elizabeth,

The true succeeders of each royal house,
By God's fair ordinance conjoin together!
And let their heirs, God, if thy will be so,
Enrich the time to come with smooth-faced peace,
With smiling plenty and fair prosperous days!
Abate the edge[1] of traitors, gracious Lord,
That would reduce[2] these bloody days again,
And make poor England weep in streams of blood!
Let them not live to taste this land's increase,
That would with treason wound this fair land's peace!
Now civil wounds are stopp'd, peace lives again:
That she may long live here, God say amen!   [*Exeunt.*]

---

1. *Abate the edge*] dull the force or spirit.
2. *reduce*] bring back.